Strange Case of Dr. Jekyll and Mr. Hyde

and

Essays in the Art of Writing

ROBERT LOUIS STEVENSON

Strange Case of
Dr. Jekyll and Mr. Hyde
and
Essays in the Art of Writing

ZULMA
classics

ZULMA
classics

JANE AUSTEN
Northanger Abbey
and Love and Freindship

WILKIE COLLINS
The Haunted Hotel
and The Dream-Woman

THOMAS HARDY
The Well-Beloved
and Alicia's Diary

NATHANIEL HAWTHORNE
Lady Eleanore's Mantle
and Other Tales of Mystery

HENRY JAMES
Italian Tales

SHERIDAN LE FANU
Carmilla

ROBERT LOUIS STEVENSON
Strange Case of Dr. Jekyll and Mr. Hyde
and Essays in the Art of Writing

OSCAR WILDE
The Picture of Dorian Gray
and The Decay of Lying

❧❧❧

Typeset in Minion and Bauer Bodoni.
Cover design: David Lee Fong.
Cover painting: *La intriga*, by Raúl Agrán (Picture Alain Mangin).
Printed in France.

ISBN 2-84304-289-5

© Zulma, 2005.
www.zulmaclassics.com

CONTENTS

Foreword   7

STRANGE CASE OF DR. JEKYLL AND MR. HYDE   9

ESSAYS IN THE ART OF WRITING   77

- Letter to a young gentleman who proposes to embrace the career of art
- Books which have influenced me
- A note on realism
- The morality of the profession of letters

FOREWORD

THE city, in the dead of night; a door yields to let out a monster —the incarnation of absolute evil. This quietly horrifying scene opens Robert Louis Stevenson's *Strange Case of Dr. Jekyll and Mr. Hyde*, a short novel which has proved just as enduring as and perhaps even more influential than *Treasure Island*. The atrocity was witnessed by Mr. Enfield, one of those London pedestrians whose like reappears in the author's *New Arabian Nights* and dazzling *Dynamiter*, written with his wife Fanny.

So what did Enfield witness? A man, of indescribable brutishness, trampling a child in an almost deserted street and then passing through the above-mentioned door, to write a cheque that will buy the parents' silence. In the labyrinth of tales that Stevenson weaves around this opening scene, the reader soon meets one of the best known and yet mysterious characters in British literature. The attacker, a certain Mr. Hyde, turns out to be a regular visitor to the eminently respectable Dr. Henry Jekyll, who has however fallen out with certain of his friends as a result of his rather questionable research. The occasional appearances of the young Edward Hyde, a forceful yet physically feeble criminal, send shock waves through this universe of mature bachelors shielded from the world by their faithful man-servants. An enquiry starts which will only reach its conclusion with the revelation of the joint destiny of Jekyll and Hyde. In the privacy of his laboratory, Dr. Jekyll had intended to separate the good in man from the evil; he decided to experiment on himself, but only succeeded in isolating the evil Other. This is Hyde, whose audacity and criminal energy are so attractive to Jekyll that he can't help frequently summoning him up—to the extent that this Other has a name, a flat in Soho, and a nocturnal life full of depravity and violence.

Thus the author invites us on a strange journey through

London and the desires of the flesh. Stevenson was born in 1850 in Edinburgh (which honours him warmly in a delightful museum shared with Walter Scott), into a family of architects and engineers; his father gave financial support to his literary ambitions. A short story and travel writer, a talented essayist, and occasional literary critic, Stevenson then wrote two hugely successful novels: *Treasure Island*, in 1883, and our *Strange Case of Dr. Jekyll and Mr. Hyde* in 1886. These were followed by a series of works that met with varying success, including another story of double identity, the fascinating *Master of Ballantrae* (1889). A vampire sibling slowly sucks the lifeblood from his brother, eventually killing him: this time Hyde has his own body, charisma, devastating charm, and, with the United States, a more extensive playing field than London.

Despite serious illness—he contracted tuberculosis at a young age—Stevenson was a passionate traveller: to France, the United States, the Mediterranean, and at the end of his life, the South Seas. He died in the Samoan Islands in 1894, not before writing the distressing *In the South Seas*, which could be considered the first ethnological treatise on the Polynesians. While Long John Silver and the Jekyll/Hyde pairing have remained vivid and relevant for readers of all ages, it is really among writers that Stevenson's reputation is unsurpassed. Arthur Conan Doyle owes him a great deal; master storytellers such as Machen, Yeats, Marcel Schwob, Calvino and Borges have all cited him as an important influence. Who else, over twenty years of a cruelly curtailed literary career, has been able to combine such precise yet dense narration—the short *Dr. Jekyll and Mr. Hyde* resembles a literary scalpel exposing the depths of the soul and the flesh—, with a devastatingly lucid critique of the author's craft, as in these masterly *Essays in the Art of Writing*? Furthermore, as Stevenson was both less arrogant and more talented than the unfortunate Jekyll, these two aspects of his work served only to enhance each other.

❧❧❧❧❧

The text of *Strange Case of Dr. Jekyll and Mr. Hyde* reproduced here is that of the first British book edition published by Longmans, Green, and Co. in 1886. A few errors in spelling and punctuation have been silently corrected.

Strange Case of
Dr. Jekyll and Mr. Hyde

TO KATHARINE DE MATTOS

It's ill to loose the bands that God decreed to bind;
Still will we be the children of the heather and the wind.
Far away from home, O it's still for you and me
That the broom is blowing bonnie in the north countrie.

STORY OF THE DOOR

MR. UTTERSON the lawyer was a man of a rugged countenance, that was never lighted by a smile; cold, scanty and embarrassed in discourse; backward in sentiment; lean, long, dusty, dreary, and yet somehow lovable. At friendly meetings, and when the wine was to his taste, something eminently human beaconed from his eye; something indeed which never found its way into his talk, but which spoke not only in these silent symbols of the after-dinner face, but more often and loudly in the acts of his life. He was austere with himself; drank gin when he was alone, to mortify a taste for vintages; and though he enjoyed the theatre, had not crossed the doors of one for twenty years. But he had an approved tolerance for others; sometimes wondering, almost with envy, at the high pressure of spirits involved in their misdeeds; and in any extremity inclined to help rather than to reprove. "I incline to Cain's heresy," he used to say quaintly: "I let my brother go to the devil in his "own way." In this character, it was frequently his fortune to be the last reputable acquaintance and the last good influence in the lives of down-going men. And to such as these, so long as they came about his chambers, he never marked a shade of change in his demeanour.

No doubt the feat was easy to Mr. Utterson; for he was undemonstrative at the best, and even his friendships seemed to be founded in a similar catholicity of good-nature. It is the mark of a modest man to accept his friendly circle ready-made from the hands of opportunity; and that was the lawyer's way. His friends were those of his own blood or those whom he had known the longest; his affections, like ivy, were the growth of time, they implied no aptness in the object. Hence, no doubt, the bond that united him to Mr. Richard Enfield, his distant kinsman, the well-known man about town. It was a nut to crack for many, what these two could see in each other or what subject they could find in common. It was reported by those who encountered them in their Sunday walks, that they said nothing, looked singularly dull, and would hail with obvious relief the appearance of a friend. For all that, the two men put the greatest store by these excursions, counted them the chief jewel of each week, and not only set aside occasions of pleasure, but even resisted the calls of business, that they might enjoy them uninterrupted.

It chanced on one of these rambles that their way led them down a by-street in a busy quarter of London. The street was small and what is called quiet, but it drove a thriving trade on the week-days. The inhabitants were all doing well, it seemed, and all emulously hoping to do better still, and laying out the surplus of their gains in coquetry; so that the shop fronts stood along that thoroughfare with an air of invitation, like rows of smiling sales-women. Even on Sunday, when it veiled its more florid charms and lay comparatively empty of passage, the street shone out in contrast to its dingy neighbourhood, like a fire in a forest; and with its freshly painted shutters, well-polished brasses, and general cleanliness and gaiety of note, instantly caught and pleased the eye of the passenger.

Two doors from one corner, on the left hand going east, the line was broken by the entry of a court; and just at that point, a certain sinister block of building thrust forward its gable on the street. It was two storeys high; showed no window, nothing but a door on the lower storey and a blind forehead of discoloured wall on the upper; and bore in every feature, the marks of prolonged and sordid negligence. The door, which was equipped with neither bell nor knocker, was blistered and distained. Tramps slouched into the recess and struck matches on the panels; children kept shop upon the steps; the schoolboy had tried his knife on the mouldings; and for close on a generation, no one had appeared to drive away these random visitors or to repair their ravages.

Mr. Enfield and the lawyer were on the other side of the by-street; but when they came abreast of the entry, the former lifted

STORY OF THE DOOR

up his cane and pointed.

"Did you ever remark that door?" he asked; and when his companion had replied in the affirmative, "It is connected in my mind," added he, "with a very odd story."

"Indeed?" said Mr. Utterson, with a slight change of voice, "and what was that?"

"Well, it was this way," returned Mr. Enfield: "I was coming home from some place at the end of the world, about three o' clock of a black winter morning, and my way lay through a part of town where there was literally nothing to be seen but lamps. Street after street, and all the folks asleep—street after street, all lighted up as if for a procession and all as empty as a church—till at last I got into that state of mind when a man listens and listens and begins to long for the sight of a policeman. All at once, I saw two figures: one a little man who was stumping along eastward at a good walk, and the other a girl of maybe eight or ten who was running as hard as she was able down a cross street. Well, sir, the two ran into one another naturally enough at the corner; and then came the horrible part of the thing; for the man trampled calmly over the child's body and left her screaming on the ground. It sounds nothing to hear, but it was hellish to see. It wasn't like a man; it was like some damned Juggernaut. I gave a view halloa, took to my heels, collared my gentleman, and brought him back to where there was already quite a group about the screaming child. He was perfectly cool and made no resistance, but gave me one look, so ugly that it brought out the sweat on me like running. The people who had turned out were the girl's own family; and pretty soon, the doctor, for whom she had been sent, put in his appearance. Well, the child was not much the worse, more frightened, according to the Sawbones; and there you might have supposed would be an end to it. But there was one curious circumstance. I had taken a loathing to my gentleman at first sight. So had the child's family, which was only natural. But the doctor's case was what struck me. He was the usual cut-and-dry apothecary, of no particular age and colour, with a strong Edinburgh accent, and about as emotional as a bagpipe. Well, sir, he was like the rest of us; every time he looked at my prisoner, I saw that Sawbones turn sick and white with the desire to kill him. I knew what was in his mind, just as he knew what was in mine; and killing being out of the question, we did the next best. We told the man we could and would make such a scandal out of this, as should make his name stink from one end of London to the other. If he had any friends or any credit, we undertook that he should lose them. And all the time, as we were pitching it in red hot, we were keeping the women off him as best we could, for they were as wild as harpies. I never saw a circle of such hateful faces; and there was the man in the middle, with a kind of black, sneering coolness—frightened too, I could see that—but carrying it off, sir, really like Satan. 'If you choose to make capital out of this accident,' said he, 'I am naturally helpless. No gentleman but wishes to avoid a scene,' says he. 'Name your figure.' Well, we screwed him up to a hundred pounds for the child's family; he would have clearly liked to stick out; but there was something about the lot of us that meant mischief, and at last he struck. The next thing was to get the money; and where do you think he carried us but to that place with the door?—whipped out a key, went in, and presently came back with the matter of ten pounds in gold and a cheque for the balance on Coutts's, drawn payable to bearer and signed with a name that I can't mention, though it's one of the points of my story, but it was a name at least very well known and often printed. The figure was stiff; but the signature was good for more than that, if it was only genuine. I took the liberty of pointing out to my gentleman that the whole business looked apocryphal, and that a man does not, in real life, walk into a cellar door at four in the morning and come out of it with another man's cheque for close upon a hundred pounds. But he was quite easy and sneering. 'Set your mind at rest,' says he, 'I will stay with you till the banks open and cash the cheque myself.' So we all set off, the doctor, and the child's father, and our friend and myself, and passed the rest of the night in my chambers; and next day, when we had breakfasted, went in a body to the bank. I gave in the cheque myself, and said I had every reason to believe it was a forgery. Not a bit of it. The cheque was genuine."

"Tut-tut," said Mr. Utterson.

"I see you feel as I do," said Mr. Enfield. "Yes, it's a bad story. For

STORY OF THE DOOR   15

my man was a fellow that nobody could have to do with, a really
damnable man; and the person that drew the cheque is the very
pink of the proprieties, celebrated too, and (what makes it worse)
one of your fellows who do what they call good. Black mail, I
suppose; an honest man paying through the nose for some of the
capers of his youth. Black Mail House is what I call that place with
the door, in consequence. Though even that, you know, is far from
explaining all," he added, and with the words fell into a vein of
musing.

From this he was recalled by Mr. Utterson asking rather
suddenly: "And you don't know if the drawer of the cheque lives
there?"

"A likely place, isn't it?" returned Mr. Enfield. "But I happen to
have noticed his address; he lives in some square or other."

"And you never asked about the—place with the door?" said
Mr. Utterson.

"No, sir: I had a delicacy," was the reply. "I feel very strongly
about putting questions; it partakes too much of the style of the
day of judgment. You start a question, and it's like starting a stone.
You sit quietly on the top of a hill; and away the stone goes, starting
others; and presently some bland old bird (the last you would have
thought of) is knocked on the head in his own back garden and the
family have to change their name. No, sir, I make it a rule of mine:
the more it looks like Queer Street, the less I ask."

" A very good rule, too," said the lawyer.

"But I have studied the place for myself," continued Mr.
Enfield." "It seems scarcely a house. There is no other door, and
nobody goes in or out of that one but, once in a great while, the
gentleman of my adventure. There are three windows looking on
the court on the first floor; none below; the windows are always
shut but they're clean. And then there is a chimney which is generally smoking; so somebody must live there. And yet it's not so sure;
for the buildings are so packed together about that court, that it's
hard to say where one ends and another begins."

The pair walked on again for a while in silence; and then,
"Enfield," said Mr. Utterson, "that's a good rule of yours."

"Yes, I think it is," returned Enfield.

16   STRANGE CASE OF DR. JEKYLL AND MR. HYDE

"But for all that," continued the lawyer, "there's one point I want to ask: I want to ask the name of that man who walked over the child."

"Well," said Mr. Enfield, "I can't see what harm it would do. It was a man of the name of Hyde."

"Hm," said Mr. Utterson. "What sort of a man is he to see?"

"He is not easy to describe. There is something wrong with his appearance; something displeasing, something downright detestable. I never saw a man I so disliked, and yet I scarce know why. He must be deformed somewhere; he gives a strong feeling of deformity, although I couldn't specify the point. He's an extraordinary looking man, and yet I really can name nothing out of the way. No, sir; I can make no hand of it; I can't describe him. And it's not want of memory; for I declare I can see him this moment."

Mr. Utterson again walked some way in silence and obviously under a weight of consideration. "You are sure he used a key?" he inquired at last.

"My dear sir…" began Enfield, surprised out of himself.

"Yes, I know," said Utterson; "I know it must seem strange. The fact is, if I do not ask you the name of the other party, it is because I know it already. You see, Richard, your tale has gone home. If you have been inexact in any point, you had better correct it."

"I think you might have warned me," returned the other, with a touch of sullenness. "But I have been pedantically exact, as you call it. The fellow had a key; and what's more, he has it still. I saw him use it, not a week ago.

Mr. Utterson sighed deeply but said never a word; and the young man presently resumed. "Here is another lesson to say nothing," said he. "I am ashamed of my long tongue. Let us make a bargain never to refer to this again."

"With all my heart," said the lawyer. "I shake hands on that, Richard."

SEARCH FOR MR. HYDE

THAT evening, Mr. Utterson came home to his bachelor house in sombre spirits and sat down to dinner without relish. It was his custom of a Sunday, when this meal was over, to sit close by the fire, a volume of some dry divinity on his reading desk, until the clock of the neighbouring church rang out the hour of twelve, when he would go soberly and gratefully to bed. On this night, however, as soon as the cloth was taken away, he took up a candle and went into his business room. There he opened his safe, took from the most private part of it a document endorsed on the envelope as Dr. Jekyll's Will, and sat down with a clouded brow to study its contents. The will was holograph, for Mr. Utterson, though he took charge of it now that it was made, had refused to lend the least assistance in the making of it; it provided not only that, in case of the decease of Henry Jekyll, M.D., D.C.L., LL.D., F.R.S., &c., all his possessions were to pass into the hands of his "friend and benefactor Edward Hyde," but that in case of Dr. Jekyll's "disappearance or unexplained absence for any period exceeding three calendar months," the said Edward Hyde should step into the said Henry Jekyll's shoes without further delay and free from any burthen or obligation, beyond the payment of a few small sums to the members of the doctor's household. This document had long been the lawyer's eyesore. It offended him both as a lawyer and as a lover of the sane and customary sides of life, to whom the fanciful was the immodest. And hitherto it was his ignorance of Mr. Hyde that had swelled his indignation; now, by a sudden turn, it was his knowledge. It was already bad enough when the name was but a name of which he could learn no more. It was worse when it began to be clothed upon with detestable attributes; and out of the shifting, insubstantial mists that had so long baffled his eye, there leaped up the sudden, definite presentment of a fiend.

"I thought it was madness," he said, as he replaced the obnoxious paper in the safe, "and now I begin to fear it is disgrace."

With that he blew out his candle, put on a great coat and set forth in the direction of Cavendish Square, that citadel of medicine, where his friend, the great Dr. Lanyon, had his house and received his crowding patients. "If anyone knows, it will be Lanyon," he had thought.

The solemn butler knew and welcomed him; he was subjected to no stage of delay, but ushered direct from the door to the dining-room where Dr. Lanyon sat alone over his wine. This was a hearty, healthy, dapper, red-faced gentleman, with a shock of hair prematurely white, and a boisterous and decided manner. At sight of Mr. Utterson, he sprang up from his chair and welcomed him with both hands. The geniality, as was the way of the man, was somewhat theatrical to the eye; but it reposed on genuine feeling. For these two were old friends, old mates both at school and college, both thorough respecters of themselves and of each other, and, what does not always follow, men who thoroughly enjoyed each other's company.

After a little rambling talk, the lawyer led up to the subject which so disagreeably preoccupied his mind.

"I suppose, Lanyon," said he, "you and I must be the two oldest friends that Henry Jekyll has?"

"I wish the friends were younger," chuckled Dr. Lanyon. "But I suppose we are. And what of that? I see little of him now."

Indeed?" said Utterson. "I thought you had a bond of common interest."

"We had," was the reply. "But it is more than ten years since Henry Jekyll became too fanciful for me. He began to go wrong, wrong in mind; and though of course I continue to take an interest in him for old sake's sake as they say, I see and I have seen devilish little of the man. Such unscientific balderdash," added the doctor, flushing suddenly purple, "would have estranged Damon and Pythias."

This little spirt of temper was somewhat of a relief to Mr.

Utterson. "They have only differed on some point of science," he thought; and being a man of no scientific passions (except in the matter of conveyancing) he even added: "It is nothing worse than that!" He gave his friend a few seconds to recover his composure, and then approached the question he had come to put. "Did you ever come across a protégé of his—one Hyde?" he asked.

"Hyde?" repeated Lanyon. "No. Never heard of him. Since my time."

That was the amount of information that the lawyer carried back with him to the great, dark bed on which he tossed to and fro, until the small hours of the morning began to grow large. It was a night of little ease to his toiling mind, toiling in mere darkness and besieged by questions.

Six o'clock struck on the bells of the church that was so conveniently near to Mr. Utterson's dwelling, and still he was digging at the problem. Hitherto it had touched him on the intellectual side alone; but now his imagination also was engaged or rather enslaved; and as he lay and tossed in the gross darkness of the night and the curtained room, Mr. Enfield's tale went by before his mind in a scroll of lighted pictures. He would be aware of the great field of lamps of a nocturnal city; then of the figure of a man walking swiftly; then of a child running from the doctor's; and then these met, and that human Juggernaut trod the child down and passed on regardless of her screams. Or else he would see a room in a rich house, where his friend lay asleep, dreaming and smiling at his dreams; and then the door of that room would be opened, the curtains of the bed plucked apart, the sleeper recalled, and lo! there would stand by his side a figure to whom power was given, and even at that dead hour, he must rise and do its bidding. The figure in these two phases haunted the lawyer all night; and if at any time he dozed over, it was but to see it glide more stealthily through sleeping houses, or move the more swiftly and still the more swiftly, even to dizziness, through wider labyrinths of lamplighted city, and at every street corner crush a child and leave her screaming. And still the figure had no face by which he might know it; even in his dreams, it had no face, or one that baffled him and melted before his eyes; and thus it was that there sprang up and grew apace in the lawyer's mind a singularly strong, almost an inordinate, curiosity to behold the features of the real Mr. Hyde. If he could but once set eyes on him, he thought the mystery would lighten and perhaps roll altogether away, as was the habit of mysterious things when well examined. He might see a reason for his friend's strange preference or bondage (call it which you please) and even for the startling clauses of the will. And at least it would be a face worth seeing: the face of a man who was without bowels of mercy: a face which had but to show itself to raise up, in the mind of the unimpressionable Enfield, a spirit of enduring hatred.

From that time forward, Mr. Utterson began to haunt the door in the by-street of shops. In the morning before office hours, at noon when business was plenty and time scarce, at night under the face of the fogged city moon, by all lights and at all hours of solitude or concourse, the lawyer was to be found on his chosen post.

"If he be Mr. Hyde," he had thought, "I shall be Mr. Seek."

And at last his patience was rewarded. It was a fine dry night; frost in the air; the streets as clean as a ballroom floor; the lamps, unshaken by any wind, drawing a regular pattern of light and shadow. By ten o'clock, when the shops were closed, the by-street was very solitary and, in spite of the low growl of London from all round, very silent. Small sounds carried far; domestic sounds out of the houses were clearly audible on either side of the roadway; and the rumour of the approach of any passenger preceded him by a long time. Mr. Utterson had been some minutes at his post, when he was aware of an odd, light footstep drawing near. In the course of his nightly patrols, he had long grown accustomed to the quaint effect with which the footfalls of a single person, while he is still a great way off, suddenly spring out distinct from the vast hum and clatter of the city. Yet his attention had never before been so sharply and decisively arrested; and it was with a strong, superstitious prevision of success that he withdrew into the entry of the court.

The steps drew swiftly nearer, and swelled out suddenly louder as they turned the end of the street. The lawyer, looking forth from the entry, could soon see what manner of man he had to deal

SEARCH FOR MR. HYDE

with. He was small and very plainly dressed, and the look of him, even at that distance, went somehow strongly against the watcher's inclination. But he made straight for the door, crossing the roadway to save time; and as he came, he drew a key from his pocket like one approaching home.

Mr. Utterson stepped out and touched him on the shoulder as he passed. "Mr. Hyde, I think?"

Mr. Hyde shrank back with a hissing intake of the breath. But his fear was only momentary; and though he did not look the lawyer in the face, he answered coolly enough: "That is my name. What do you want?"

"I see you are going in," returned the lawyer. "I am an old friend of Dr. Jekyll's—Mr. Utterson of Gaunt Street—you must have heard my name; and meeting you so conveniently, I thought you might admit me."

"You will not find Dr. Jekyll; he is from home," replied Mr. Hyde, blowing in the key. And then suddenly, but still without looking up, "How did you know me?" he asked.

"On your side," said Mr. Utterson, "will you do me a favour?"

"With pleasure," replied the other. "What shall it be?"

"Will you let me see your face?" asked the lawyer.

Mr. Hyde appeared to hesitate, and then, as if upon some sudden reflection, fronted about with an air of defiance; and the pair stared at each other pretty fixedly for a few seconds. "Now I shall know you again," said Mr. Utterson. "It may be useful."

"Yes," returned Mr. Hyde, "it is as well we have, met; and à propos, you should have my address." And he gave a number of a street in Soho.

"Good God!" thought Mr. Utterson, "can he too have been thinking of the will?" But he kept his feelings to himself and only grunted in acknowledgment of the address.

"And now," said the other, "how did you know me?"

"By description," was the reply.

"Whose description?"

"We have common friends," said Mr. Utterson.

"Common friends?" echoed Mr. Hyde, a little hoarsely." Who are they?"

"Jekyll, for instance," said the lawyer.

"He never told you," cried Mr. Hyde, with a flush of anger." I did not think you would have lied."

"Come," said Mr. Utterson, "that is not fitting language."

The other snarled aloud into a savage laugh; and the next moment, with extraordinary quickness, he had unlocked the door and disappeared into the house.

The lawyer stood awhile when Mr. Hyde had left him, the picture of disquietude. Then he began slowly to mount the street, pausing every step or two and putting his hand to his brow like a man in mental perplexity. The problem he was thus debating as he walked, was one of a class that is rarely solved. Mr. Hyde was pale and dwarfish, he gave an impression of deformity without any nameable malformation, he had a displeasing smile, he had borne himself to the lawyer with a sort of murderous mixture of timidity and boldness, and he spoke with a husky, whispering and some-what broken voice; all these were points against him, but not all of these together could explain the hitherto unknown disgust, loathing and fear with which Mr. Utterson regarded him. "There must be something else," said the perplexed gentleman. "There *is* something more, if I could find a name for it. God bless me, the man seems hardly human! Something troglodytic, shall we say? or can it be the old story of Dr. Fell? or is it the mere radiance of a foul soul that thus transpires through, and transfigures, its clay continent? The last, I think; for O my poor old Harry Jekyll, if ever I read Satan's signature upon a face, it is on that of your new friend."

Round the corner from the by-street, there was a square of ancient, handsome houses, now for the most part decayed from their high estate and let in flats and chambers to all sorts and conditions of men: map-engravers, architects, shady lawyers, and the agents of obscure enterprises. One house, however, second from the corner, was still occupied entire; and at the door of this, which wore a great air of wealth and comfort, though it was now plunged in darkness except for the fan-light, Mr. Utterson stopped and knocked. A well-dressed, elderly servant opened the door.

"Is Dr. Jekyll at home, Poole?" asked the lawyer.

"I will see, Mr. Utterson," said Poole, admitting the visitor, as he

SEARCH FOR MR. HYDE

spoke, into a large, low-roofed, comfortable hall, paved with flags, warmed (after the fashion of a country house) by a bright, open fire, and furnished with costly cabinets of oak. "Will you wait here by the fire, sir? or shall I give you a light in the dining-room?"

"Here, thank you," said the lawyer, and he drew near and leaned on the tall fender. This hall, in which he was now left alone, was a pet fancy of his friend the doctor's; and Utterson himself was wont to speak of it as the pleasantest room in London. But to-night there was a shudder in his blood; the face of Hyde sat heavy on his memory; he felt (what was rare with him) a nausea and distaste of life; and in the gloom of his spirits, he seemed to read a menace in the flickering of the firelight on the polished cabinets and the uneasy starting of the shadow on the roof. He was ashamed of his relief, when Poole presently returned to announce that Dr. Jekyll was gone out.

"I saw Mr. Hyde go in by the old dissecting room door, Poole," he said. "Is that right, when Dr. Jekyll is from home?"

"Quite right, Mr. Utterson, sir," replied the servant. "Mr. Hyde has a key."

"Your master seems to repose a great deal of trust in that young man, Poole," resumed the other musingly.

"Yes, sir, he do indeed," said Poole. "We have all orders to obey him."

"I do not think I ever met Mr. Hyde?" asked Utterson.

"O, dear no, sir. He never *dines* here," replied the butler. "Indeed we see very little of him on this side of the house; he mostly comes and goes by the laboratory."

"Well, good night, Poole."

"Good night, Mr. Utterson."

And the lawyer set out homeward with a very heavy heart. "Poor Harry Jekyll," he thought, "my mind misgives me he is in deep waters! He was wild when he was young; a long while ago to be sure; but in the law of God, there is no statute of limitations. Ay, it must be that; the ghost of some old sin, the cancer of some concealed disgrace: punishment coming, *pede claudo*, years after memory has forgotten and self-love condoned the fault." And the lawyer, scared by the thought, brooded awhile on his own past, groping in all the corners of memory, lest by chance some Jack-in-the-Box of an old iniquity should leap to light there. His past was fairly blameless; few men could read the rolls of their life with less apprehension; yet he was humbled to the dust by the many ill things he had done, and raised up again into a sober and fearful gratitude by the many that he had come so near to doing, yet avoided. And then by a return on his former subject, he conceived a spark of hope. "This Master Hyde, if he were studied," thought he, "must have secrets of his own: black secrets, by the look of him; secrets compared to which poor Jekyll's worst would be like sunshine. Things cannot continue as they are. It turns me cold to think of this creature stealing like a thief to Harry's bedside; poor Harry, what a wakening! And the danger of it; for if this Hyde suspects the existence of the will, he may grow impatient to inherit. Ay, I must put my shoulder to the wheel—if Jekyll will but let me," he added, "if Jekyll will only let me." For once more he saw before his mind's eye, as clear as a transparency, the strange clauses of the will.

DR. JEKYLL WAS QUITE AT EASE

❧❦❧

A FORTNIGHT later, by excellent good fortune, the doctor gave one of his pleasant dinners to some five or six old cronies, all intelligent, reputable men and all judges of good wine; and Mr. Utterson so contrived that he remained behind after the others had departed. This was no new arrangement, but a thing that had befallen many scores of times. Where Utterson was liked, he was liked well. Hosts loved to detain the dry lawyer, when the light-hearted and the loose-tongued had already their foot on the threshold; they liked to sit awhile in his unobtrusive company, practising for solitude; sobering their minds in the man's rich silence after the expense and strain of gaiety. To this rule, Dr. Jekyll was no exception; and as he now sat on the opposite side of the fire—a large, well-made, smooth-faced man of fifty, with something of a slyish cast perhaps, but every mark of capacity and kindness—you could see by his looks that he cherished for Mr. Utterson a sincere and warm affection.

"I have been wanting to speak to you, Jekyll," began the latter. "You know that will of yours?"

A close observer might have gathered that the topic was distasteful; but the doctor carried it off gaily. "My poor Utterson," said he, "you are unfortunate in such a client. I never saw a man so distressed as you were by my will; unless it were that hide-bound pedant, Lanyon, at what he called my scientific heresies. O, I know he's a good fellow—you needn't frown—an excellent fellow, and I always mean to see more of him; but a hide-bound pedant for all that; an ignorant, blatant pedant. I was never more disappointed in any man than Lanyon."

"You know I never approved of it," pursued Utterson, ruthlessly disregarding the fresh topic.

"My will? Yes, certainly, I know that," said the doctor, a trifle sharply. "You have told me so."

"Well, I tell you so again," continued the lawyer. "I have been learning something of young Hyde."

The large handsome face of Dr. Jekyll grew pale to the very lips, and there came a blackness about his eyes. "I do not care to hear more," said he. "This is a matter I thought we had agreed to drop."

"What I heard was abominable," said Utterson.

"It can make no change. You do not understand my position," returned the doctor, with a certain incoherency of manner. "I am painfully situated, Utterson; my position is a very strange—a very strange one. It is one of those affairs that cannot be mended by talking."

"Jekyll," said Utterson, "you know me: I am a man to be trusted. Make a clean breast of this in confidence; and I make no doubt I can get you out of it."

"My good Utterson," said the doctor, "this is very good of you, this is downright good of you, and I cannot find words to thank you in. I believe you fully; I would trust you before any man alive, ay, before myself, if I could make the choice; but indeed it isn't what you fancy; it is not so bad as that; and just to put your good heart at rest, I will tell you one thing: the moment I choose, I can be rid of Mr. Hyde. I give you my hand upon that; and I thank you again and again; and I will just add one little word, Utterson, that I'm sure you'll take in good part: this is a private matter, and I beg of you to let it sleep."

Utterson reflected a little, looking in the fire.

"I have no doubt you are perfectly right," he said at last, getting to his feet.

"Well, but since we have touched upon this business, and for the last time I hope," continued the doctor, "there is one point I should like you to understand. I have really a very great interest in poor Hyde. I know you have seen him; he told me so; and I fear he was rude. But I do sincerely take a great, a very great interest in that young man; and if I am taken away, Utterson, I wish you to promise me that you will bear with him and get his rights for him. I think you would, if you knew all; and it would be a weight off my mind if you would promise."

"I can't pretend that I shall ever like him," said the lawyer.

"I don't ask that," pleaded Jekyll, laying his hand upon the other's arm; "I only ask for justice; I only ask you to help him for my sake, when I am no longer here."

Utterson heaved an irrepressible sigh. "Well," said he. "I promise."

THE CAREW MURDER CASE

～～～～～

NEARLY a year later, in the month of October, 18—, London was startled by a crime of singular ferocity and rendered all the more notable by the high position of the victim. The details were few and startling. A maid servant living alone in a house not far from the river, had gone upstairs to bed about eleven. Although a fog rolled over the city in the small hours, the early part of the night was cloudless, and the lane, which the maid's window over-looked, was brilliantly lit by the full moon. It seems she was romantically given, for she sat down upon her box, which stood immediately under the window, and fell into a dream of musing. Never (she used to say, with streaming tears, when she narrated that experience) never had she felt more at peace with all men or thought more kindly of the world. And as she so sat she became aware of an aged and beautiful gentleman with white hair, drawing near along the lane; and advancing to meet him, another and very small gentleman, to whom at first she paid less attention. When they had come within speech (which was just under the maid's eyes) the older man bowed and accosted the other with a very pretty manner of politeness. It did not seem as if the subject of his address were of great importance; indeed, from his pointing, it sometimes appeared as if he were only inquiring his way; but the moon shone on his face as he spoke, and the girl was pleased to watch it, it seemed to breathe such an innocent and old-world kindness of disposition, yet with something high too, as of a well-founded self-content. Presently her eye wandered to the other, and she was surprised to recognise in him a certain Mr. Hyde, who had once visited her master and for whom she had conceived a dislike. He had in his hand a heavy cane, with which he was trifling; but he answered never a word, and seemed to listen with an ill-contained impatience. And then all of a sudden he broke out in a great flame of anger, stamping with his foot, brandishing the cane, and carrying on (as the maid described it) like a madman. The old gentleman took a step back, with the air of one very much surprised and a trifle hurt; and at that Mr. Hyde broke out of all bounds and clubbed him to the earth. And next moment, with ape-like fury, he was trampling his victim under foot, and hailing down a storm of blows, under which the bones were audibly shattered and the body jumped upon the roadway. At the horror of these sights and sounds, the maid fainted.

It was two o'clock when she came to herself and called for the police. The murderer was gone long ago; but there lay his victim in the middle of the lane, incredibly mangled. The stick with which the deed had been done, although it was of some rare and very tough and heavy wood, had broken in the middle under the stress of this insensate cruelty; and one splintered half had rolled in the neighbouring gutter—the other, without doubt, had been carried away by the murderer. A purse and a gold watch were found upon the victim; but no cards or papers, except a sealed and stamped envelope, which he had been probably carrying to the post, and which bore the name and address of Mr. Utterson.

This was brought to the lawyer the next morning, before he was out of bed; and he had no sooner seen it, and been told the circumstances, than he shot out a solemn lip. "I shall say nothing till I have seen the body," said he; "this may be very serious. Have the kindness to wait while I dress." And with the same grave countenance he hurried through his breakfast and drove to the police station, whither the body had been carried. As soon as he came into the cell, he nodded.

"Yes," said he, "I recognise him. I am sorry to say that this is Sir Danvers Carew."

"Good God, sir," exclaimed the officer, "is it possible?" And the next moment his eye lighted up with professional ambition. "This will make a deal of noise," he said. "And perhaps you can help us to the man." And he briefly narrated what the maid had seen, and showed the broken stick.

THE CAREW MURDER CASE   29

Mr. Utterson had already quailed at the name of Hyde; but when the stick was laid before him, he could doubt no longer: broken and battered as it was, he recognised it for one that he had himself presented many years before to Henry Jekyll.

"Is this Mr. Hyde a person of small stature?" he inquired.

"Particularly small and particularly wicked-looking, is what the maid calls him," said the officer.

Mr. Utterson reflected; and then, raising his head, "If you will come with me in my cab," he said, "I think I can take you to his house."

It was by this time about nine in the morning, and the first fog of the season. A great chocolate-coloured pall lowered over heaven, but the wind was continually charging and routing these embattled vapours; so that as the cab crawled from street to street, Mr. Utterson beheld a marvellous number of degrees and hues of twilight; for here it would be dark like the back-end of evening; and there would be a glow of a rich, lurid brown, like the light of some strange conflagration; and here, for a moment, the fog would be quite broken up, and a haggard shaft of daylight would glance in between the swirling wreaths. The dismal quarter of Soho seen under these changing glimpses, with its muddy ways, and slatternly passengers, and its lamps, which had never been extinguished or had been kindled afresh to combat this mournful reinvasion of darkness, seemed, in the lawyer's eyes, like a district of some city in a nightmare. The thoughts of his mind, besides, were of the gloomiest dye; and when he glanced at the companion of his drive, he was conscious of some touch of that terror of the law and the law's officers, which may at times assail the most honest.

As the cab drew up before the address indicated, the fog lifted a little and showed him a dingy street, a gin palace, a low French eating house, a shop for the retail of penny numbers and twopenny salads, many ragged children huddled in the doorways, and many women of different nationalities passing out, key in hand, to have a morning glass; and the next moment the fog settled down again upon that part, as brown as umber, and cut him off from his blackguardly surroundings. This was the home of Henry Jekyll's favourite; of a man who was heir to a quarter of a million sterling.

An ivory-faced and silvery-haired old woman opened the door. She had an evil face, smoothed by hypocrisy; but her manners were excellent. Yes, she said, this was Mr. Hyde's, but he was not at home; he had been in that night very late, but had gone away again in less than an hour; there was nothing strange in that; his habits were very irregular, and he was often absent; for instance, it was nearly two months since she had seen him till yesterday.

"Very well then, we wish to see his rooms," said the lawyer; and when the woman began to declare it was impossible, "I had better tell you who this person is," he added. "This is Inspector Newcomen of Scotland Yard."

A flash of odious joy appeared upon the woman's face. "Ah!" said she, "he is in trouble! What has he done?"

Mr. Utterson and the inspector exchanged glances. "He don't seem a very popular character," observed the latter. "And now, my good woman, just let me and this gentleman have a look about us."

In the whole extent of the house, which but for the old woman remained otherwise empty, Mr. Hyde had only used a couple of rooms; but these were furnished with luxury and good taste. A closet was filled with wine; the plate was of silver, the napery elegant; a good picture hung upon the walls, a gift (as Utterson supposed) from Henry Jekyll, who was much of a connoisseur; and the carpets were of many plies and agreeable in colour. At this moment, however, the rooms bore every mark of having been recently and hurriedly ransacked; clothes lay about the floor, with their pockets inside out; lockfast drawers stood open; and on the hearth there lay a pile of grey ashes, as though many papers had been burned. From these embers the inspector disinterred the butt end of a green cheque book, which had resisted the action of the fire; the other half of the stick was found behind the door; and as this clinched his suspicions, the officer declared himself delighted. A visit to the bank, where several thousand pounds were found to be lying to the murderer's credit, completed his gratification.

"You may depend upon it, sir," he told Mr. Utterson: "I have him in my hand. He must have lost his head, or he never would have left the stick or, above all, burned the cheque book. Why, money's life to the man. We have nothing to do but wait for him at the bank, and get out the handbills."

This last, however, was not so easy of accomplishment; for Mr. Hyde had numbered few familiars—even the master of the servant maid had only seen him twice; his family could nowhere be traced; he had never been photographed; and the few who could describe him differed widely, as common observers will. Only on one point, were they agreed; and that was the haunting sense of unexpressed deformity with which the fugitive impressed his beholders.

INCIDENT OF THE LETTER

It was late in the afternoon, when Mr. Utterson found his way to Dr. Jekyll's door, where he was at once admitted by Poole, and carried down by the kitchen offices and across a yard which had once been a garden, to the building which was indifferently known as the laboratory or the dissecting rooms. The doctor had bought the house from the heirs of a celebrated surgeon; and his own tastes being rather chemical than anatomical, had changed the destination of the block at the bottom of the garden. It was the first time that the lawyer had been received in that part of his friend's quarters; and he eyed the dingy, windowless structure with curiosity, and gazed round with a distasteful sense of strangeness as he crossed the theatre, once crowded with eager students and now lying gaunt and silent, the tables laden with chemical apparatus, the floor strewn with crates and littered with packing straw, and the light falling dimly through the foggy cupola. At the further end, a flight of stairs mounted to a door covered with red baize; and through this, Mr. Utterson was at last received into the doctor's cabinet. It was a large room, fitted round with glass presses, furnished, among other things, with a cheval-glass and a business table, and looking out upon the court by three dusty windows barred with iron. The fire burned in the grate; a lamp was set lighted on the chimney shelf, for even in the houses the fog began to lie thickly; and there, close up to the warmth, sat Dr. Jekyll, looking deadly sick. He did not rise to meet his visitor, but held out a cold hand and bade him welcome in a changed voice.

"And now," said Mr. Utterson, as soon as Poole had left them, "you have heard the news?"

The doctor shuddered. "They were crying it in the square," he said. "I heard them in my dining room."

"One word," said the lawyer. "Carew was my client, but so are you, and I want to know what I am doing. You have not been mad enough to hide this fellow?"

"Utterson, I swear to God," cried the doctor, "I swear to God I will never set eyes on him again. I bind my honour to you that I am done with him in this world. It is all at an end. And indeed he does not want my help; you do not know him as I do; he is safe, he is quite safe; mark my words, he will never more be heard of."

The lawyer listened gloomily; he did not like his friend's feverish manner. "You seem pretty sure of him," said he; "and for your sake, I hope you may be right. If it came to a trial, your name might appear."

"I am quite sure of him," replied Jekyll; "I have grounds for certainty that I cannot share with anyone. But there is one thing on which you may advise me. I have—I have received a letter; and I am at a loss whether I should show it to the police. I should like to leave it in your hands, Utterson; you would judge wisely, I am sure; I have so great a trust in you."

"You fear, I suppose, that it might lead to his detection?" asked the lawyer.

"No," said the other. "I cannot say that I care what becomes of Hyde; I am quite done with him. I was thinking of my own character, which this hateful business has rather exposed."

Utterson ruminated awhile; he was surprised at his friend's selfishness, and yet relieved by it. "Well," said he, at last, "let me see the letter."

The letter was written in an odd, upright hand and signed

INCIDENT OF THE LETTER 33

"Edward Hyde": and it signified, briefly enough, that the writer's benefactor, Dr. Jekyll, whom he had long so unworthily repaid for a thousand generosities, need labour under no alarm for his safety as he had means of escape on which he placed a sure dependence. The lawyer liked this letter well enough; it put a better colour on the intimacy than he had looked for; and he blamed himself for some of his past suspicions.

"Have you the envelope?" he asked.

"I burned it," replied Jekyll," before I thought what I was about. But it bore no postmark. The note was handed in."

"Shall I keep this and sleep upon it?" asked Utterson.

"I wish you to judge for me entirely," was the reply. "I have lost confidence in myself."

"Well, I shall consider," returned the lawyer. "And now one word more: it was Hyde who dictated the terms in your will about that disappearance?"

The doctor seemed seized with a qualm of faintness; he shut his mouth tight and nodded.

"I knew it," said Utterson. "He meant to murder you. You have had a fine escape."

"I have had what is far more to the purpose," returned the doctor solemnly: "I have had a lesson—O God, Utterson, what a lesson I have had!" And he covered his face for a moment with his hands.

On his way out, the lawyer stopped and had a word or two with Poole. "By the by," said he, "there was a letter handed in to-day: what was the messenger like?" But Poole was positive nothing had come except by post; "and only circulars by that," he added.

This news sent off the visitor with his fears renewed. Plainly the letter had come by the laboratory door; possibly, indeed, it had been written in the cabinet; and if that were so, it must be differently judged, and handled with the more caution. The newsboys, as he went, were crying themselves hoarse along the footways: "Special edition. Shocking murder of an M.P." That was the funeral oration of one friend and client; and he could not help a certain apprehension lest the good name of another should be sucked down in the eddy of the scandal. It was, at least, a ticklish decision that he had to make; and self-reliant as he was by habit, he began to cherish a longing for advice. It was not to be had directly; but perhaps, he thought, it might be fished for.

Presently after, he sat on one side of his own hearth, with Mr. Guest, his head clerk, upon the other, and midway between, at a nicely calculated distance from the fire, a bottle of a particular old wine that had long dwelt unsunned in the foundations of his house. The fog still slept on the wing above the drowned city, where the lamps glimmered like carbuncles; and through the muffle and smother of these fallen clouds, the procession of the town's life was still rolling in through the great arteries with a sound as of a mighty wind. But the room was gay with firelight. In the bottle the acids were long ago resolved; the imperial dye had softened with time, as the colour grows richer in stained windows; and the glow of hot autumn afternoons on hillside vineyards, was ready to be set free and to disperse the fogs of London. Insensibly the lawyer melted. There was no man from whom he kept fewer secrets than Mr. Guest; and he was not always sure that he kept as many as he meant. Guest had often been on business to the doctor's; he knew Poole; he could scarce have failed to hear of Mr. Hyde's familiarity about the house; he might draw conclusions: was it not as well, then, that he should see a letter which put that mystery to rights? and above all since Guest, being a great student and critic of handwriting, would consider the step natural and obliging? The clerk, besides, was a man of counsel; he would scarce read so strange a document without dropping a remark; and by that remark Mr. Utterson might shape his future course.

"This is a sad business about Sir Danvers," he said.

"Yes, sir, indeed. It has elicited a great deal of public feeling," returned Guest. "The man, of course, was mad."

"I should like to hear your views on that," replied Utterson. "I have a document here in his handwriting; it is between ourselves, for I scarce know what to do about it; it is an ugly business at the best. But there it is; quite in your way: a murderer's autograph."

Guest's eyes brightened, and he sat down at once and studied it with passion. "No, sir," he said; "not mad; but it is an odd hand."

"And by all accounts a very odd writer," added the lawyer.

Just then the servant entered with a note.

"Is that from Dr. Jekyll, sir?" inquired the clerk. "I thought I knew the writing. Anything private, Mr. Utterson?"

"Only an invitation to dinner. Why? do you want to see it?"

"One moment. I thank you, sir;" and the clerk laid the two sheets of paper alongside and sedulously compared their contents. "Thank you, sir," he said at last, returning both; "it's a very interesting autograph."

There was a pause, during which Mr. Utterson struggled with himself. "Why did you compare them, Guest?" he inquired suddenly.

"Well, sir," returned the clerk, "there's a rather singular resemblance; the two hands are in many points identical: only differently sloped."

"Rather quaint," said Utterson.

"It is, as you say, rather quaint," returned Guest.

"I wouldn't speak of this note, you know," said the master.

"No, sir," said the clerk. "I understand."

But no sooner was Mr. Utterson alone that night, than he locked the note into his safe where it reposed from that time forward. "What!" he thought. "Henry Jekyll forge for a murderer!" And his blood ran cold in his veins.

REMARKABLE INCIDENT OF DR. LANYON

TIME ran on; thousands of pounds were offered in reward, for the death of Sir Danvers was resented as a public injury; but Mr. Hyde had disappeared out of the ken of the police as though he had never existed. Much of his past was unearthed, indeed, and all disreputable: tales came out of the man's cruelty, at once so callous and violent, of his vile life, of his strange associates, of the hatred that seemed to have surrounded his career; but of his present whereabouts, not a whisper. From the time he had left the house in Soho on the morning of the murder, he was simply blotted out; and gradually, as time drew on, Mr. Utterson began to recover from the hotness of his alarm, and to grow more at quiet with himself. The death of Sir Danvers was, to his way of thinking, more than paid for by the disappearance of Mr. Hyde. Now that that evil influence had been withdrawn, a new life began for Dr. Jekyll. He came out of his seclusion, renewed relations with his friends, became once more their familiar guest and entertainer; and whilst he had always been known for charities, he was now no less distinguished for religion. He was busy, he was much in the open air, he did good; his face seemed to open and brighten, as if with an inward consciousness of service; and for more than two months, the doctor was at peace.

On the 8th of January Utterson had dined at the doctor's with a small party; Lanyon had been there; and the face of the host had looked from one to the other as in the old days when the trio were inseparable friends. On the 12th, and again on the 14th, the door was shut against the lawyer. "The doctor was confined to the house," Poole said, "and saw no one." On the 15th, he tried again, and was again refused; and having now been used for the last two months to see his friend almost daily, he found this return of solitude to weight upon his spirits. The fifth night, he had in Guest to dine with him; and the sixth he betook himself to Dr. Lanyon's.

There at least he was not denied admittance; but when he came in, he was shocked at the change which had taken place in the doctor's appearance. He had his death-warrant written legibly upon his face. The rosy man had grown pale; his flesh had fallen away; he was visibly balder and older; and yet it was not so much these tokens of a swift physical decay that arrested the lawyer's notice, as a look in the eye and quality of manner that seemed to testify to some deep-seated terror of the mind. It was unlikely that the doctor should fear death; and yet that was what Utterson was tempted to suspect. "Yes," he thought, "he is a doctor, he must know his own state and that his days are counted; and the knowledge is more than he can bear." And yet when Utterson remarked

REMARKABLE INCIDENT OF DR. LANYON   37

on his ill-looks, it was with an air of great firmness that Lanyon declared himself a doomed man.

"I have had a shock," he said, "and I shall never recover. It is a question of weeks. Well, life has been pleasant; I liked it; yes, sir, I used to like it. I sometimes think if we knew all, we should be more glad to get away."

"Jekyll is ill, too," observed Utterson. "Have you seen him?"

But Lanyon's face changed, and he held up a trembling hand. "I wish to see or hear no more of Dr. Jekyll," he said in a loud, unsteady voice. "I am quite done with that person; and I beg that you will spare me any allusion to one whom I regard as dead."

"Tut-tut," said Mr. Utterson; and then after a considerable pause, "Can't I do anything?" he inquired. "We are three very old friends, Lanyon; we shall not live to make others."

"Nothing can be done," returned Lanyon; "ask himself."

"He will not see me," said the lawyer.

"I am not surprised at that," was the reply.

"Some day, Utterson, after I am dead, you may perhaps come to learn the right and wrong of this. I cannot tell you. And in the meantime, if you can sit and talk with me of other things, for God's sake, stay and do so; but if you cannot keep clear of this accursed topic, then, in God's name, go, for I cannot bear it."

As soon as he got home, Utterson sat down and wrote to Jekyll, complaining of his exclusion from the house, and asking the cause of this unhappy break with Lanyon; and the next day brought him a long answer, often very pathetically worded, and sometimes darkly mysterious in drift. The quarrel with Lanyon was incurable. "I do not blame our old friend," Jekyll wrote, "but I share his view that we must never meet. I mean from henceforth to lead a life of extreme seclusion; you must not be surprised, nor must you doubt my friendship, if my door is often shut even to you. You must suffer me to go my own dark way. I have brought on myself a punishment and a danger that I cannot name. If I am the chief of sinners, I am the chief of sufferers also. I could not think that this earth contained a place for sufferings and terrors so unmanning; and you can do but one thing, Utterson, to lighten this destiny, and that is to respect my silence." Utterson was amazed; the dark influence of Hyde had been withdrawn, the doctor had returned to his old tasks and amities; a week ago, the prospect had smiled with every promise of a cheerful and an honoured age; and now in a moment, friendship, and peace of mind and the whole tenor of his life were wrecked. So great and unprepared a change pointed to madness; but in view of Lanyon's manner and words, there must lie for it some deeper ground.

A week afterwards Dr. Lanyon took to his bed, and in something less than a fortnight he was dead. The night after the funeral, at which he had been sadly affected, Utterson locked the door of his business room, and sitting there by the light of a melancholy candle, drew out and set before him an envelope addressed by the hand and sealed with the seal of his dead friend. "PRIVATE: for the hands of G. J. Utterson ALONE and in case of his predecease *to be destroyed unread*," so it was emphatically superscribed; and the lawyer dreaded to behold the contents. "I have buried one friend to-day," he thought: "what if this should cost me another?" And then he condemned the fear as a disloyalty, and broke the seal. Within there was another enclosure, likewise sealed, and marked upon the cover as "not to be opened till the death or disappearance of Dr. Henry Jekyll." Utterson could not trust his eyes. Yes, it was disappearance; here again, as in the mad will which he had long ago restored to its author, here again were the idea of a disappearance and the name of Henry Jekyll bracketed. But in the will, that idea had sprung from the sinister suggestion of the man Hyde; it was set there with a purpose all too plain and horrible. Written by the hand of Lanyon, what should it mean? A great curiosity came on the trustee, to disregard the prohibition and dive at once to the bottom of these mysteries; but professional honour and faith to his dead friend were stringent obligations; and the packet slept in the inmost corner of his private safe.

It is one thing to mortify curiosity, another to conquer it; and it may be doubted if, from that day forth, Utterson desired the society of his surviving friend with the same eagerness. He thought of him kindly; but his thoughts were disquieted and fearful. He went to call indeed; but he was perhaps relieved to be denied admittance; perhaps, in his heart, he preferred to speak with Poole upon the doorstep and surrounded by the air and sounds of the open city, rather than to be admitted into that house of voluntary bondage, and to sit and speak with its inscrutable recluse. Poole had, indeed, no very pleasant news to communicate. The doctor, it appeared, now more than ever confined himself to the cabinet over the laboratory, where he would sometimes even sleep; he was out of spirits, he had grown very silent, he did not read; it seemed as if he had something on his mind. Utterson became so used to the unvarying character of these reports, that he fell off little by little in the frequency of his visits.

INCIDENT AT THE WINDOW

~~~~~~

IT chanced on Sunday, when Mr. Utterson was on his usual walk with Mr. Enfield, that their way lay once again through the by-street; and that when they came in front of the door, both stopped to gaze on it.

"Well," said Enfield, "that story's at an end at least. We shall never see more of Mr. Hyde."

"I hope not," said Utterson. "Did I ever tell you that I once saw him, and shared your feeling of repulsion?"

"It was impossible to do the one without the other," returned Enfield. "And by the way what an ass you must have thought me, not to know that this was a back way to Dr. Jekyll's! It was partly your own fault that I found it out, even when I did."

"So you found it out, did you?" said Utterson.

"But if that be so, we may step into the court and take a look at the windows. To tell you the truth, I am uneasy about poor Jekyll; and even outside, I feel as if the presence of a friend might do him good."

The court was very cool and a little damp, and full of premature twilight, although the sky, high up overhead, was still bright with sunset. The middle one of the three windows was half way open; and sitting close beside it, taking the air with an infinite sadness of mien, like some disconsolate prisoner, Utterson saw Dr. Jekyll.

"What! Jekyll!" he cried. "I trust you are better."

"I am very low, Utterson," replied the doctor drearily, "very low. It will not last long, thank God."

"You stay too much indoors," said the lawyer. "You should be out, whipping up the circulation like Mr. Enfield and me. (This is my cousin—Mr. Enfield—Dr. Jekyll.) Come now; get your hat and take a quick turn with us."

"You are very good," sighed the other. "I should like to very much; but no, no, no, it is quite impossible; I dare not. But indeed, Utterson, I am very glad to see you; this is really a great pleasure; I would ask you and Mr. Enfield up, but the place is really not fit."

"Why then," said the lawyer, good-naturedly, "the best thing we can do is to stay down here and speak with you from where we are."

"That is just what I was about to venture to propose," returned the doctor with a smile. But the words were hardly uttered, before the smile was struck out of his face and succeeded by an expression of such abject terror and despair, as froze the very blood of the two gentlemen below. They saw it but for a glimpse, for the window was instantly thrust down; but that glimpse had been sufficient, and they turned and left the court without a word. In silence, too, they traversed the by-street; and it was not until they had come into a neighbouring thoroughfare, where even upon a Sunday there were still some stirrings of life, that Mr. Utterson at last turned and looked at his companion. They were both pale; and there was an answering horror in their eyes.

"God forgive us, God forgive us," said Mr. Utterson.

But Mr. Enfield only nodded his head very seriously and walked on once more in silence.

THE LAST NIGHT

MR. UTTERSON was sitting by his fireside one evening after dinner, when he was surprised to receive a visit from Poole.

"Bless me, Poole, what brings you here?" he cried; and then taking a second look at him, "What ails you?" he added, "is the doctor ill?"

"Mr. Utterson," said the man, "there is something wrong."

"Take a seat, and here is a glass of wine for you," said the lawyer. "Now, take your time, and tell me plainly what you want."

"You know the doctor's ways, sir," replied Poole, "and how he shuts himself up. Well, he's shut up again in the cabinet; and I don't like it, sir—I wish I may die if I like it. Mr. Utterson, sir, I'm afraid."

"Now, my good man," said the lawyer, "be explicit. What are you afraid of?"

"I've been afraid for about a week," returned Poole, doggedly disregarding the question, "and I can bear it no more."

The man's appearance amply bore out his words; his manner was altered for the worse; and except for the moment when he had first announced his terror, he had not once looked the lawyer in the face. Even now, he sat with the glass of wine untasted on his knee, and his eyes directed to a corner of the floor. "I can bear it no more," he repeated.

"Come," said the lawyer, "I see you have some good reason, Poole; I see there is something seriously amiss. Try to tell me what it is."

"I think there's been foul play," said Poole, hoarsely.

"Foul play!" cried the lawyer, a good deal frightened and rather inclined to be irritated in consequence. "What foul play? What does the man mean?"

"I daren't say, sir" was the answer; "but will you come along with me and see for yourself?"

Mr. Utterson's only answer was to rise and get his hat and great coat; but he observed with wonder the greatness of the relief that appeared upon the butler's face, and perhaps with no less, that the wine was still untasted when he set it down to follow.

It was a wild, cold, seasonable night of March, with a pale moon, lying on her back as though the wind had tilted her, and a flying wrack of the most diaphanous and lawny texture. The wind made talking difficult, and flecked the blood into the face. It seemed to have swept the streets unusually bare of passengers, besides; for Mr. Utterson thought he had never seen that part of London so deserted. He could have wished it otherwise; never in his life had he been conscious of so sharp a wish to see and touch his fellow-creatures; for struggle as he might, there was borne in upon his mind a crushing anticipation of calamity. The square, when they got there, was all full of wind and dust, and the thin trees in the garden were lashing themselves along the railing. Poole, who had kept all the way a pace or two ahead, now pulled up in the middle of the pavement, and in spite of the biting weather, took off his hat and mopped his brow with a red pocket-handker-chief. But for all the hurry of his coming, these were not the dews of exertion that he wiped away, but the moisture of some stran-gling anguish; for his face was white and his voice, when he spoke, harsh and broken.

"Well, sir," he said, "here we are, and God grant there be nothing wrong."

"Amen, Poole," said the lawyer.

Thereupon the servant knocked in a very guarded manner; the door was opened on the chain; and a voice asked from within, "Is that you, Poole?"

"It's all right," said Poole. "Open the door."

The hall, when they entered it, was brightly lighted up; the fire was built high; and about the hearth the whole of the servants, men and women, stood huddled together like a flock of sheep. At the sight of Mr. Utterson, the housemaid broke into hysterical whimpering; and the cook, crying out "Bless God! it's Mr.

THE LAST NIGHT   43

Utterson," ran forward as if to take him in her arms.

"What, what? Are you all here?" said the lawyer peevishly. "Very irregular, very unseemly; your master would be far from pleased."

"They're all afraid," said Poole.

Blank silence followed, no one protesting; only the maid lifted up her voice and now wept loudly.

"Hold your tongue!" Poole said to her, with a ferocity of accent that testified to his own jangled nerves; and indeed, when the girl had so suddenly raised the note of her lamentation, they had all started and turned towards the inner door with faces of dreadful expectation. "And now," continued the butler, addressing the knife-boy, "reach me a candle, and we'll get this through hands at once." And then he begged Mr. Utterson to follow him, and led the way to the back garden.

"Now, sir," said he, "you come as gently as you can. I want you to hear, and I don't want you to be heard. And see here, sir, if by any chance he was to ask you in, don't go."

Mr. Utterson's nerves, at this unlooked-for termination, gave a jerk that nearly threw him from his balance; but he recollected his courage and followed the butler into the laboratory building and through the surgical theatre, with its lumber of crates and bottles, to the foot of the stair. Here Poole motioned him to stand on one side and listen; while he himself, setting down the candle and making a great and obvious call on his resolution, mounted the steps and knocked with a somewhat uncertain hand on the red baize of the cabinet door.

"Mr. Utterson, sir, asking to see you, "he called; and even as he did so, once more violently signed to the lawyer to give ear.

A voice answered from within: "Tell him I cannot see anyone," it said complainingly.

"Thank you, sir," said Poole, with a note of something like triumph in his voice; and taking up his candle, he led Mr. Utterson back across the yard and into the great kitchen, where the fire was out and the beetles were leaping on the floor.

"Sir," he said, looking Mr. Utterson in the eyes, "was that my master's voice?"

"It seems much changed," replied the lawyer, very pale, but

44   STRANGE CASE OF DR. JEKYLL AND MR. HYDE

giving look for look.

"Changed? Well, yes, I think so," said the butler. "Have I been twenty years in this man's house, to be deceived about his voice? No, sir; master's made away with; he was made away with, eight days ago, when we heard him cry out upon the name of God; and *who's* in there instead of him, and *why* it stays there, is a thing that cries to Heaven, Mr. Utterson!"

"This is a very strange tale, Poole; this is rather a wild tale, my man," said Mr. Utterson, biting his finger. "Suppose it were as you suppose, supposing Dr. Jekyll to have been—well, murdered, what could induce the murderer to stay? That won't hold water; it doesn't commend itself to reason."

"Well, Mr. Utterson, you are a hard man to satisfy, but I'll do it yet," said Poole. "All this last week (you must know) him, or it, or whatever it is that lives in that cabinet, has been crying night and day for some sort of medicine and cannot get it to his mind. It was sometimes his way—the master's, that is—to write his orders on a sheet of paper and throw it on the stair. We've had nothing else this week back; nothing but papers, and a closed door, and the very meals left there to be smuggled in when nobody was looking. Well, sir, every day, ay, and twice and thrice in the same day, there have been orders and complaints, and I have been sent flying to all the wholesale chemists in town. Every time I brought the stuff back, there would be another paper telling me to return it, because it was not pure, and another order to a different firm. This drug is wanted bitter bad, sir, whatever for."

"Have you any of these papers?" asked Mr. Utterson.

Poole felt in his pocket and handed out a crumpled note, which the lawyer, bending nearer to the candle, carefully examined. Its contents ran thus: "Dr. Jekyll presents his compliments to Messrs. Maw. He assures them that their last sample is impure and quite useless for his present purpose. In the year 18—, Dr. J. purchased a somewhat large quantity from Messrs. M. He now begs them to search with the most sedulous care, and should any of the same quality be left, to forward it to him at once. Expense is no consideration. The importance of this to Dr. J. can hardly be exaggerated." So far the letter had run composedly enough, but here with

THE LAST NIGHT   45

a sudden splutter of the pen, the writer's emotion had broken loose. "For God's sake," he had added, "find me some of the old."

"This is a strange note," said Mr. Utterson; and then sharply, "How do you come to have it open?"

"The man at Maw's was main angry, sir, and he threw it back to me like so much dirt," returned Poole.

"This is unquestionably the doctor's hand, do you know?" resumed the lawyer.

"I thought it looked like it," said the servant rather sulkily; and then, with another voice, "But what matters hand of write? " he said. "I've seen him!"

"Seen him?" repeated Mr. Utterson. "Well?"

"That's it!" said Poole. "It was this way. I came suddenly into the theatre from the garden. It seems he had slipped out to look for this drug or whatever it is; for the cabinet door was open, and there he was at the far end of the room digging among the crates. He looked up when I came in, gave a kind of cry, and whipped upstairs into the cabinet. It was but for one minute that I saw him, but the hair stood upon my head like quills. Sir, if that was my master, why had he a mask upon his face? If it was my master, why did he cry out like a rat, and run from me? I have served him long enough. And then ... " the man paused and passed his hand over his face.

"These are all very strange circumstances," said Mr. Utterson, "but I think I begin to see daylight. Your master, Poole, is plainly seized with one of those maladies that both torture and deform the sufferer; hence, for aught I know, the alteration of his voice; hence the mask and the avoidance of his friends; hence his eagerness to find this drug, by means of which the poor soul retains some hope of ultimate recovery—God grant that he be not deceived! There is my explanation; it is sad enough, Poole, ay, and appalling to consider; but it is plain and natural, hangs well together, and delivers us from all exorbitant alarms."

"Sir," said the butler, turning to a sort of mottled pallor, "that thing was not my master, and there's the truth. My master"—here he looked round him and began to whisper—"is a tall, fine build of a man, and this was more of a dwarf." Utterson attempted to protest. "O, sir," cried Poole, "do you think I do not know my master after twenty years? do you think I do not know where his head comes to in the cabinet door, where I saw him every morning of my life? No, sir, that thing in the mask was never Dr. Jekyll— God knows what it was, but it was never Dr. Jekyll; and it is the belief of my heart that there was murder done."

"Poole," replied the lawyer, "if you say that, it will become my duty to make certain. Much as I desire to spare your master's feelings, much as I am puzzled by this note which seems to prove him to be still alive, I shall consider it my duty to break in that door."

"Ah, Mr. Utterson, that's talking!" cried the butler.

"And now comes the second question," resumed Utterson: "Who is going to do it?"

"Why, you and me, sir," was the undaunted reply.

"That is very well said," returned the lawyer; "and whatever comes of it, I shall make it my business to see you are no loser."

"There is an axe in the theatre," continued Poole, "and you might take the kitchen poker for yourself."

The lawyer took that rude but weighty instrument into his hand, and balanced it. "Do you know, Poole," he said, looking up, "that you and I are about to place ourselves in a position of some peril?"

"You may say so, sir, indeed," returned the butler.

"It is well, then, that we should be frank," said the other. "We both think more than we have said; let us make a clean breast. This masked figure that you saw, did you recognise it?"

"Well, sir, it went so quick, and the creature was so doubled up, that I could hardly swear to that," was the answer. "But if you mean, was it Mr. Hyde?—why, yes, I think it was! You see, it was much of the same bigness; and it had the same quick light way with it; and then who else could have got in by the laboratory door? You have not forgot, sir that at the time of the murder he had still the key with him? But that's not all. I don't know, Mr. Utterson, if ever you met this Mr. Hyde?"

"Yes," said the lawyer, "I once spoke with him."

"Then you must know as well as the rest of us that there was something queer about that gentleman—something that gave a

THE LAST NIGHT   47

man a turn—I don't know rightly how to say it, sir, beyond this: that you felt it in your marrow kind of cold and thin."

"I own I felt something of what you describe," said Mr. Utterson.

"Quite so, sir," returned Poole. "Well, when that masked thing like a monkey jumped from among the chemicals and whipped into the cabinet, it went down my spine like ice. O, I know it's not evidence, Mr. Utterson. I'm book-learned enough for that; but a man has his feelings, and I give you my Bible-word it was Mr. Hyde!"

"Ay, ay," said the lawyer. "My fears incline to the same point. Evil, I fear, founded—evil was sure to come—of that connection. Ay, truly, I believe you; I believe poor Harry is killed; and I believe his murderer (for what purpose, God alone can tell) is still lurking in his victim's room. Well, let our name be vengeance. Call Bradshaw."

The footman came at the summons, very white and nervous.

"Pull yourself together, Bradshaw," said the lawyer. "This suspense, I know, is telling upon all of you; but it is now our intention to make an end of it. Poole, here, and I are going to force our way into the cabinet. If all is well, my shoulders are broad enough to bear the blame. Meanwhile, lest anything should really be amiss, or any malefactor seek to escape by the back, you and the boy must go round the corner with a pair of good sticks, and take your post at the laboratory door. We give you ten minutes, to get to your stations."

As Bradshaw left, the lawyer looked at his watch. "And now, Poole, let us get to ours," he said; and taking the poker under his arm, led the way into the yard. The scud had banked over the moon, and it was now quite dark. The wind, which only broke in puffs and draughts into that deep well of building, tossed the light of the candle to and fro about their steps, until they came into the shelter of the theatre, where they sat down silently to wait. London hummed solemnly all around; but nearer at hand, the stillness was only broken by the sound of a footfall moving to and fro along the cabinet floor.

"So it will walk all day, sir," whispered Poole; "ay, and the better

48   STRANGE CASE OF DR. JEKYLL AND MR. HYDE

part of the night. Only when a new sample comes from the chemist, there's a bit of a break. Ah, it's an ill-conscience that's such an enemy to rest! Ah, sir, there's blood foully shed in every step of it! But hark again, a little closer—put your heart in your ears, Mr. Utterson, and tell me, is that the doctor's foot?"

The steps fell lightly and oddly, with a certain swing, for all they went so slowly; it was different indeed from the heavy creaking tread of Henry Jekyll. Utterson sighed. "Is there never anything else?" he asked.

Poole nodded. "Once," he said. "Once I heard it weeping!"

"Weeping? how that?" said the lawyer, conscious of a sudden chill of horror.

"Weeping like a woman or a lost soul," said the butler. "I came away with that upon my heart, that I could have wept too."

But now the ten minutes drew to an end. Poole disinterred the axe from under a stack of packing straw; the candle was set upon the nearest table to light them to the attack; and they drew near with bated breath to where that patient foot was still going up and down, up and down, in the quiet of the night.

"Jekyll," cried Utterson, with a loud voice, "I demand to see you." He paused a moment, but there came no reply. "I give you fair warning, our suspicions are aroused, and I must and shall see you," he resumed; "if not by fair means, then by foul—if not of your consent, then by brute force!"

"Utterson," said the voice, "for God's sake, have mercy!"

Ah, that's not Jekyll's voice—it's Hyde's!" cried Utterson. "Down with the door, Poole!"

Poole swung the axe over his shoulder; the blow shook the building, and the red baize door leaped against the lock and hinges. A dismal screech, as of mere animal terror, rang from the cabinet. Up went the axe again, and again the panels crashed and the frame bounded; four times the blow fell; but the wood was tough and the fittings were of excellent workmanship; and it was not until the fifth, that the lock burst in sunder and the wreck of the door fell inwards on the carpet.

The besiegers, appalled by their own riot and the stillness that had succeeded, stood back a little and peered in. There lay the

THE LAST NIGHT 49

cabinet before their eyes in the quiet lamplight, a good fire glowing and chattering on the hearth, the kettle singing its thin strain, a drawer or two open, papers neatly set forth on the business table, and nearer the fire, the things laid out for tea: the quietest room, you would have said, and, but for the glazed presses full of chemicals, the most commonplace that night in London.

Right in the midst there lay the body of a man sorely contorted and still twitching. They drew near on tiptoe, turned it on its back and beheld the face of Edward Hyde. He was dressed in clothes far too large for him, clothes of the doctor's bigness; the cords of his face still moved with a semblance of life, but life was quite gone; and by the crushed phial in the hand and the strong smell of kernels that hung upon the air, Utterson knew that he was looking on the body of a self-destroyer.

"We have come too late," he said sternly, "whether to save or punish. Hyde is gone to his account; and it only remains for us to find the body of your master."

The far greater proportion of the building was occupied by the theatre, which filled almost the whole ground story and was lighted from above, and by the cabinet, which formed an upper story at one end and looked upon the court. A corridor joined the theatre to the door on the by-street; and with this, the cabinet communicated separately by a second flight of stairs. There were besides a few dark closets and a spacious cellar. All these they now thoroughly examined. Each closet needed but a glance, for all were empty and all, by the dust that fell from their doors, had stood long unopened. The cellar, indeed, was filled with crazy lumber, mostly dating from the times of the surgeon who was Jekyll's predecessor; but even as they opened the door they were advertised of the uselessness of further search, by the fall of a perfect mat of cobweb which had for years sealed up the entrance. Nowhere was there any trace of Henry Jekyll, dead or alive.

Poole stamped on the flags of the corridor. "He must be buried here," he said, hearkening to the sound.

"Or he may have fled," said Utterson, and he turned to examine the door in the by-street. It was locked; and lying near by on the flags, they found the key, already stained with rust.

50   STRANGE CASE OF DR. JEKYLL AND MR. HYDE

"This does not look like use," observed the lawyer.

"Use!" echoed Poole. "Do you not see, sir, it is broken? much as if a man had stamped on it."

"Ay," continued Utterson," and the fractures, too, are rusty." The two men looked at each other with a scare. "This is beyond me, Poole," said the lawyer. "Let us go back to the cabinet."

They mounted the stair in silence, and still with an occasional awe struck glance at the dead body, proceeded more thoroughly to examine the contents of the cabinet. At one table, there were traces of chemical work, various measured heaps of some white salt being laid on glass saucers, as though for an experiment in which the unhappy man had been prevented.

"That is the same drug that I was always bringing him," said Poole; and even as he spoke, the kettle with a startling noise boiled over.

This brought them to the fireside, where the easy chair was drawn cosily up, and the tea things stood ready to the sitter's elbow, the very sugar in the cup. There were several books on a shelf; one lay beside the tea things open, and Utterson was amazed to find it a copy of a pious work, for which Jekyll had several times expressed a great esteem, annotated, in his own hand, with startling blasphemies.

Next, in the course of their review of the chamber, the searchers came to the cheval glass, into whose depths they looked with an involuntary horror. But it was so turned as to show them nothing but the rosy glow playing on the roof, the fire sparkling in a hundred repetitions along the glazed front of the presses, and their own pale and fearful countenances stooping to look in.

"This glass have seen some strange things, sir," whispered Poole.

"And surely none stranger than itself," echoed the lawyer in the same tones. "For what did Jekyll"—he caught himself up at the word with a start, and then conquering the weakness—"what could Jekyll want with it?" he said.

"You may say that!" said Poole.

Next they turned to the business table. On the desk among the neat array of papers, a large envelope was uppermost, and bore, in

THE LAST NIGHT   51

the doctor's hand, the name of Mr. Utterson. The lawyer unsealed
it, and several enclosures fell to the floor. The first was a will, drawn
in the same eccentric terms as the one which he had returned six
months before, to serve as a testament in case of death and as a
deed of gift in case of disappearance; but, in place of the name of
Edward Hyde, the lawyer, with indescribable amazement, read the
name of Gabriel John Utterson. He looked at Poole, and then back
at the paper, and last of all at the dead malefactor stretched upon
the carpet.

"My head goes round," he said. "He has been all these days in
possession; he had no cause to like me; he must have raged to see
himself displaced; and he has not destroyed this document."

He caught up the next paper; it was a brief note in the doctor's
hand and dated at the top. "O Poole!" the lawyer cried, "he was
alive and here this day. He cannot have been disposed of in so short
a space, he must be still alive, he must have fled! And then, why
fled? and how? and in that case, can we venture to declare this
suicide? O, we must be careful. I foresee that we may yet involve
your master in some dire catastrophe."

"Why don't you read it, sir?" asked Poole.

"Because I fear," replied the lawyer solemnly. " God grant I have
no cause for it!" And with that he brought the paper to his eyes and
read as follows:

"MY DEAR UTTERSON,—When this shall fall into your hands,
I shall have disappeared, under what circumstances I have not the
penetration to foresee, but my instinct and all the circumstances of
my nameless situation tell me that the end is sure and must be
early. Go then, and first read the narrative which Lanyon warned
me he was to place in your hands; and if you care to hear more,
turn to the confession of

"Your unworthy and unhappy friend,

"HENRY JEKYLL."

"There was a third enclosure?" asked Utterson.

"Here, sir," said Poole, and gave into his hands a considerable
packet sealed in several places.

The lawyer put it in his pocket. "I would say nothing of this paper. If your master has fled or is dead, we may at least save his credit. It is now ten; I must go home and read these documents in quiet; but I shall be back before midnight, when we shall send for the police."

They went out, locking the door of the theatre behind them; and Utterson, once more leaving the servants gathered about the fire in the hall, trudged back to his office to read the two narratives in which this mystery was now to be explained.

DR. LANYON'S NARRATIVE

ON the ninth of January, now four days ago, I received by the evening delivery a registered envelope, addressed in the hand of my colleague and old school-companion, Henry Jekyll. I was a good deal surprised by this; for we were by no means in the habit of correspondence; I had seen the man, dined with him, indeed, the night before; and I could imagine nothing in our intercourse that should justify the formality of registration. The contents increased my wonder; for this is how the letter ran:

"10th December, 18 —

"DEAR LANYON,—You are one of my oldest friends; and although we may have differed at times on scientific questions, I cannot remember, at least on my side, any break in our affection. There was never a day when, if you had said to me, 'Jekyll, my life, my honour, my reason, depend upon you,' I would not have sacrificed my fortune or my left hand to help you. Lanyon, my life, my honour, my reason, are all at your mercy; if you fail me to-night, I am lost. You might suppose, after this preface, that I am

DR. LANYON'S NARRATIVE

going to ask you for something dishonourable to grant. Judge for yourself.

"I want you to postpone all other engagements for to-night—ay, even if you were summoned to the bedside of an emperor; to take a cab, unless your carriage should be actually at the door; and with this letter in your hand for consultation, to drive straight to my house. Poole, my butler, has his orders; you will find him waiting your arrival with a locksmith. The door of my cabinet is then to be forced; you are to go in alone; to open the glazed press (letter E) on the left hand, breaking the lock if it be shut; and to draw out, *with all its contents as they stand*, the fourth drawer from the top or (which is the same thing) the third from the bottom. In my extreme distress of mind, I have a morbid fear of misdirecting you; but even if I am in error, you may know the right drawer by its contents: some powders, a phial and a paper book. This drawer I beg of you to carry back with you to Cavendish Square exactly as it stands.

"That is the first part of the service: now for the second. You should be back, if you set out at once on the receipt of this, long before midnight; but I will leave you that amount of margin, not only in the fear of one of those obstacles that can neither be prevented nor foreseen, but because an hour when your servants are in bed is to be preferred for what will then remain to do. At midnight, then, I have to ask you to be alone in your consulting room, to admit with your own hand into the house a man who will present himself in my name, and to place in his hands the drawer that you will have brought with you from my cabinet. Then you will have played your part and earned my gratitude completely. Five minutes afterwards, if you insist upon an explanation, you will have understood that these arrangements are of capital importance; and that by the neglect of one of them, fantastic as they must appear, you might have charged your conscience with my death or the shipwreck of my reason.

"Confident as I am that you will not trifle with this appeal, my heart sinks and my hand trembles at the bare thought of such a possibility. Think of me at this hour, in a strange place, labouring under a blackness of distress that no fancy can exaggerate, and yet well aware that, if you will but punctually serve me, my troubles will roll away like a story that is told. Serve me, my dear Lanyon, and save

"Your friend,
"H. J."

"P. S. I had already sealed this up when a fresh terror struck upon my soul. It is possible that the post office may fail me, and this letter not come into your hands until to-morrow morning. In that case, dear Lanyon, do my errand when it shall be most convenient for you in the course of the day; and once more expect my messenger at midnight. It may then already be too late; and if that night passes without event, you will know that you have seen the last of Henry Jekyll."

Upon the reading of this letter, I made sure my colleague was insane; but till that was proved beyond the possibility of doubt, I felt bound to do as he requested. The less I understood of this farrago, the less I was in a position to judge of its importance; and an appeal so worded could not be set aside without a grave responsibility. I rose accordingly from table, got into a hansom, and drove straight to Jekyll's house. The butler was awaiting my arrival; he had received by the same post as mine a registered letter of instruction, and had sent at once for a locksmith and a carpenter. The tradesmen came while we were yet speaking; and we moved in a body to old Dr. Denman's surgical theatre, from which (as you are doubtless aware) Jekyll's private cabinet is most conveniently entered. The door was very strong, the lock excellent; the carpenter avowed he would have great trouble and have to do much damage, if force were to be used; and the locksmith was near despair. But this last was a handy fellow, and after two hours' work, the door stood open. The press marked E was unlocked; and I took out the drawer, had it filled up with straw and tied in a sheet, and returned with it to Cavendish Square.

Here I proceeded to examine its contents. The powders were neatly enough made up, but not with the nicety of the dispensing chemist; so that it was plain they were of Jekyll's private manufac-

DR. LANYON'S NARRATIVE

ture; and when I opened one of the wrappers, I found what seemed to me a simple, crystalline salt of a white colour. The phial, to which I next turned my attention, might have been about half-full of a blood-red liquor, which was highly pungent to the sense of smell and seemed to me to contain phosphorus and some volatile ether. At the other ingredients, I could make no guess. The book was an ordinary version book and contained little but a series of dates. These covered a period of many years, but I observed that the entries ceased nearly a year ago and quite abruptly. Here and there a brief remark was appended to a date, usually no more than a single word: "double" occurring perhaps six times in a total of several hundred entries; and once very early in the list and followed by several marks of exclamation, "total failure!!!" All this, though it whetted my curiosity, told me little that was definite. Here were a phial of some tincture, a paper of some salt, and the record of a series of experiments that had led (like too many of Jekyll's investigations) to no end of practical usefulness. How could the presence of these articles in my house affect either the honour, the sanity, or the life of my flighty colleague? If his messenger could go to one place, why could he not go to another? And even granting some impediment, why was this gentleman to be received by me in secret? The more I reflected, the more convinced I grew that I was dealing with a case of cerebral disease: and though I dismissed my servants to bed, I loaded an old revolver that I might be found in some posture of self-defence.

Twelve o'clock had scarce rung out over London, ere the knocker sounded very gently on the door. I went myself at the summons, and found a small man crouching against the pillars of the portico.

"Are you come from Dr. Jekyll?" I asked.

He told me "yes" by a constrained gesture; and when I had bidden him enter, he did not obey me without a searching backward glance into the darkness of the square. There was a policeman not far off, advancing with his bull's eye open; and at the sight, I thought my visitor started and made greater haste.

These particulars struck me, I confess, disagreeably; and as I followed him into the bright light of the consulting room, I kept my hand ready on my weapon. Here, at last, I had a chance of clearly seeing him. I had never set eyes on him before, so much was certain. He was small, as I have said; I was struck besides with the shocking expression of his face, with his remarkable combination of great muscular activity and great apparent debility of constitution, and—last but not least—with the odd, subjective disturbance caused by his neighbourhood. This bore some resemblance to incipient rigor, and was accompanied by a marked sinking of the pulse. At the time, I set it down to some idiosyncratic, personal distaste, and merely wondered at the acuteness of the symptoms; but I have since had reason to believe the cause to lie much deeper in the nature of man, and to turn on some nobler hinge than the principle of hatred.

This person (who had thus, from the first moment of his entrance, struck in me what I can only describe as a disgustful curiosity) was dressed in a fashion that would have made an ordinary person laughable: his clothes, that is to say, although they were of rich and sober fabric, were enormously too large for him in every measurement—the trousers hanging on his legs and rolled up to keep them from the ground, the waist of the coat below his haunches, and the collar sprawling wide upon his shoulders. Strange to relate, this ludicrous accoutrement was far from moving me to laughter. Rather, as there was something abnormal and misbegotten in the very essence of the creature that now faced me—something seizing, surprising and revolting—this fresh disparity seemed but to fit in with and to reinforce it; so that to my interest in the man's nature and character, there was added a curiosity as to his origin, his life, his fortune and status in the world.

These observations, though they have taken so great a space to be set down in, were yet the work of a few seconds. My visitor was, indeed, on fire with sombre excitement.

"Have you got it?" he cried. "Have you got it?" And so lively was his impatience that he even laid his hand upon my arm and sought to shake me.

I put him back, conscious at his touch of a certain icy pang along my blood. "Come, sir," said I. "You forget that I have not yet

DR. LANYON'S NARRATIVE

the pleasure of your acquaintance. Be seated, if you please." And I showed him an example, and sat down myself in my customary seat and with as fair an imitation of my ordinary manner to a patient, as the lateness of the hour, the nature of my preoccupations, and the horror I had of my visitor, would suffer me to muster.

"I beg your pardon, Dr. Lanyon," he replied civilly enough. "What you say is very well founded; and my impatience has shown its heels to my politeness. I come here at the instance of your colleague, Dr. Henry Jekyll, on a piece of business of some moment; and I understood ..." he paused and put his hand to his throat, and I could see, in spite of his collected manner, that he was wrestling against the approaches of the hysteria—"I understood, a drawer ..."

But here I took pity on my visitor's suspense, and some perhaps on my own growing curiosity.

"There it is, sir," said I, pointing to the drawer, where it lay on the floor behind a table and still covered with the sheet.

He sprang to it, and then paused, and laid his hand upon his heart; I could hear his teeth grate with the convulsive action of his jaws; and his face was so ghastly to see that I grew alarmed both for his life and reason.

"Compose yourself," said I.

He turned a dreadful smile to me, and as if with the decision of despair, plucked away the sheet. At sight of the contents, he uttered one loud sob of such immense relief that I sat petrified. And the next moment, in a voice that was already fairly well under control, "Have you a graduated glass?" he asked.

I rose from my place with something of an effort and gave him what he asked.

He thanked me with a smiling nod, measured out a few minims of the red tincture and added one of the powders. The mixture, which was at first of a reddish hue, began, in proportion as the crystals melted, to brighten in colour, to effervesce audibly, and to throw off small fumes of vapour. Suddenly and at the same moment, the ebullition ceased and the compound changed to a dark purple, which faded again more slowly to a watery green. My visitor, who had watched these metamorphoses with a keen eye, smiled, set down the glass upon the table, and then turned and looked upon me with an air of scrutiny.

"And now," said he, "to settle what remains. Will you be wise? will you be guided? will you suffer me to take this glass in my hand and to go forth from your house without further parley? or has the greed of curiosity too much command of you? Think before you answer, for it shall be done as you decide. As you decide, you shall be left as you were before, and neither richer nor wiser, unless the sense of service rendered to a man in mortal distress may be counted as a kind of riches of the soul. Or, if you shall so prefer to choose, a new province of knowledge and new avenues to fame and power shall be laid open to you, here, in this room, upon the instant; and your sight shall be blasted by a prodigy to stagger the unbelief of Satan."

"Sir," said I, affecting a coolness that I was far from truly possessing, "you speak enigmas, and you will perhaps not wonder that I hear you with no very strong impression of belief. But I have gone too far in the way of inexplicable services to pause before I see the end."

"It is well," replied my visitor. "Lanyon, you remember your vows: what follows is under the seal of our profession. And now, you who have so long been bound to the most narrow and material views, you who have denied the virtue of transcendental medicine, you who have derided your superiors—behold!"

He put the glass to his lips and drank at one gulp. A cry followed; he reeled, staggered, clutched at the table and held on, staring with injected eyes, gasping with open mouth; and as I looked there came, I thought, a change—he seemed to swell—his face became suddenly black and the features seemed to melt and alter—and the next moment, I had sprung to my feet and leaped back against the wall, my arm raised to shield me from that prodigy, my mind submerged in terror.

"O God!" I screamed, and "O God!" again and again; for there before my eyes—pale and shaken, and half fainting, and groping before him with his hands, like a man restored from death—there stood Henry Jekyll!

What he told me in the next hour, I cannot bring my mind to set on paper. I saw what I saw, I heard what I heard, and my soul sickened at it; and yet now when that sight has faded from my eyes, I ask myself if I believe it, and I cannot answer. My life is shaken to its roots; sleep has left me; the deadliest terror sits by me at all hours of the day and night; I feel that my days are numbered, and that I must die; and yet I shall die incredulous. As for the moral turpitude that man unveiled to me, even with tears of penitence, I cannot, even in memory, dwell on it without a start of horror. I will say but one thing, Utterson, and that (if you can bring your mind to credit it) will be more than enough. The creature who crept into my house that night was, on Jekyll's own confession, known by the name of Hyde and hunted for in every corner of the land as the murderer of Carew.

HASTIE LANYON.

HENRY JEKYLL'S FULL STATEMENT OF THE CASE

I WAS born in the year 18— to a large fortune, endowed besides with excellent parts, inclined by nature to industry, fond of the respect of the wise and good among my fellow-men, and thus, as might have been supposed, with every guarantee of an honourable and distinguished future. And indeed the worst of my faults was a certain impatient gaiety of disposition, such as has made the happiness of many, but such as I found it hard to reconcile with my imperious desire to carry my head high, and wear a more than commonly grave countenance before the public. Hence it came about that I concealed my pleasures; and that when I reached years of reflection, and began to look round me and take stock of my progress and position in the world, I stood already committed to a profound duplicity of life. Many a man would have even blazoned such irregularities as I was guilty of; but from the high views that I had set before me, I regarded and hid them with an almost morbid sense of shame. It was thus rather the exacting nature of my aspirations than any particular degradation in my faults, that made me what I was and, with even a deeper trench than in the majority of men, severed in me those provinces of good and ill which divide and compound man's dual nature. In this case, I was driven to reflect deeply and inveterately on that hard law of life, which lies at the root of religion and is one of the most plentiful springs of distress. Though so profound a double-dealer, I was in no sense a hypocrite; both sides of me were in dead earnest; I was no more myself when I laid aside restraint and plunged in shame, than when I laboured, in the eye of day, at the furtherance of knowledge or the relief of sorrow and suffering. And it chanced that the direction of my scientific studies, which led wholly towards the mystic and the transcendental, reacted and shed a strong light on this consciousness of the perennial war among my members. With every day, and from both sides of my intelligence, the moral and the intellectual, I thus drew steadily nearer to that truth, by whose partial discovery I have been doomed to such a dreadful shipwreck: that man is not truly one, but truly two. I say two, because the state of my own knowledge does not pass beyond that point. Others will follow, others will outstrip me on the same lines; and I hazard the guess that man will be ultimately known for a mere polity of multifarious, incongruous, and independent denizens. I for my part, from the nature of my life, advanced infallibly in one direction and in one direction only. It was on the moral side, and in my own person, that I learned to recognise the thorough and primitive duality of man; I saw that, of the two natures that contended in the field of my consciousness, even if I could rightly be said to be either, it was only because I was radically both; and from an early date, even before the course of my scientific discoveries had begun to suggest the most naked possibility of such a miracle, I had learned to dwell with pleasure, as a beloved day-dream, on the thought of the separation of these elements. If each, I told myself, could but be housed in separate identities, life would be relieved of all that was unbearable; the

HENRY JEKYLL'S FULL STATEMENT OF THE CASE 61

unjust might go his way delivered from the aspirations, and remorse of his more upright twin; and the just could walk steadfastly and securely on his upward path, doing the good things in which he found his pleasure, and no longer exposed to disgrace and penitence by the hands of this extraneous evil. It was the curse of mankind that these incongruous faggots were thus bound together—that in the agonised womb of consciousness, these polar twins should be continuously struggling. How, then, were they dissociated?

I was so far in my reflections when, as I have said, a side light began to shine upon the subject from the laboratory table. I began to perceive more deeply than it has ever yet been stated, the trembling immateriality, the mist-like transience, of this seemingly so solid body in which we walk attired. Certain agents I found to have the power to shake and to pluck back that fleshly vestment, even as a wind might toss the curtains of a pavilion. For two good reasons, I will not enter deeply into this scientific branch of my confession. First, because I have been made to learn that the doom and burthen of our life is bound forever on man's shoulders, and when the attempt is made to cast it off, it but returns upon us with more unfamiliar and more awful pressure. Second, because as my narrative will make, alas! too evident, my discoveries were incomplete. Enough, then, that I not only recognised my natural body for the mere aura and effulgence of certain of the powers that made up my spirit, but managed to compound a drug by which these powers should be dethroned from their supremacy, and a second form and countenance substituted, none the less natural to me because they were the expression, and bore the stamp, of lower elements in my soul.

I hesitated long before I put this theory to the test of practice. I knew well that I risked death; for any drug that so potently controlled and shook the very fortress of identity, might by the least scruple of an overdose or at the least inopportunity in the moment of exhibition, utterly blot out that immaterial tabernacle which I looked to it to change. But the temptation of a discovery so singular and profound, at last overcame the suggestions of alarm. I had long since prepared my tincture; I purchased at once, from a firm of wholesale chemists, a large quantity of a particular salt which I knew, from my experiments, to be the last ingredient required; and late one accursed night, I compounded the elements, watched them boil and smoke together in the glass, and when the ebullition had subsided, with a strong glow of courage, drank off the potion.

The most racking pangs succeeded: a grinding in the bones, deadly nausea, and a horror of the spirit that cannot be exceeded at the hour of birth or death. Then these agonies began swiftly to subside, and I came to myself as if out of a great sickness. There was something strange in my sensations, something indescribably new and, from its very novelty, incredibly sweet. I felt younger, lighter, happier in body; within I was conscious of a heady reck-lessness, a current of disordered sensual images running like a mill race in my fancy, a solution of the bonds of obligation, an unknown but not an innocent freedom of the soul. I knew myself, at the first breath of this new life, to be more wicked, tenfold more wicked, sold a slave to my original evil; and the thought, in that moment, braced and delighted me like wine. I stretched out my hands, exulting in the freshness of these sensations; and in the act, I was suddenly aware that I had lost in stature.

There was no mirror, at that date, in my room; that which stands beside me as I write, was brought there later on and for the very purpose of these transformations. The night, however, was far gone into the morning—the morning, black as it was, was nearly ripe for the conception of the day—the inmates of my house were locked in the most rigorous hours of slumber; and I determined, flushed as I was with hope and triumph, to venture in my new shape as far as to my bedroom. I crossed the yard, wherein the constellations looked down upon me, I could have thought, with wonder, the first creature of that sort that their unsleeping vigil-ance had yet disclosed to them; I stole through the corridors, a stranger in my own house; and coming to my room, I saw for the first time the appearance of Edward Hyde.

I must here speak by theory alone, saying not that which I know, but that which I suppose to be most probable. The evil side of my nature, to which I had now transferred the stamping efficacy, was less robust and less developed than the good which I had just deposed. Again, in the course of my life, which had been, after all, nine tenths a life of effort, virtue and control, it had been much less exercised and much less exhausted. And hence, as I think, it came about that Edward Hyde was so much smaller, slighter and younger than Henry Jekyll. Even as good shone upon the countenance of the one, evil was written broadly and plainly on the face of the other. Evil besides (which I must still believe to be the lethal side of man) had left on that body an imprint of deformity and decay. And yet when I looked upon that ugly idol in the glass, I was conscious of no repugnance, rather of a leap of welcome. This, too, was myself. It seemed natural and human. In my eyes it bore a livelier image of the spirit, it seemed more express and single, than the imperfect and divided countenance, I had been hitherto accustomed to call mine. And in so far I was doubtless right. I have observed that when I wore the semblance of Edward Hyde, none could come near to me at first without a visible misgiving of the flesh. This, as I take it, was because all human beings, as we meet them, are commingled out of good and evil: and Edward Hyde, alone in the ranks of mankind, was pure evil.

I lingered but a moment at the mirror: the second and conclusive experiment had yet to be attempted; it yet remained to be seen if I had lost my identity beyond redemption and must flee before daylight from a house that was no longer mine; and hurrying back to my cabinet, I once more prepared and drank the cup, once more suffered the pangs of dissolution, and came to myself once more with the character, the stature, and the face of Henry Jekyll.

That night I had come to the fatal cross roads. Had I approached my discovery in a more noble spirit, had I risked the experiment while under the empire of generous or pious aspirations, all must have been otherwise, and from these agonies of death and birth, I had come forth an angel instead of a fiend. The drug had no discriminating action; it was neither diabolical nor divine; it but shook the doors of the prison house of my disposition; and like the captives of Philippi, that which stood within ran forth. At that time my virtue slumbered; my evil, kept awake by ambition, was alert and swift to seize the occasion; and the thing that was projected was Edward Hyde. Hence, although I had now two characters as well as two appearances, one was wholly evil, and the other was still the old Henry Jekyll, that incongruous compound of whose reformation and improvement I had already learned to despair. The movement was thus wholly toward the worse.

Even at that time, I had not yet conquered my aversion to the dryness of a life of study. I would still be merrily disposed at times; and as my pleasures were (to say the least) undignified, and I was not only well known and highly considered, but growing towards the elderly man, this incoherency of my life was daily growing more unwelcome. It was on this side that my new power tempted me until I fell in slavery. I had but to drink the cup, to doff at once the body of the noted professor, and to assume, like a thick cloak, that of Edward Hyde. I smiled at the notion; it seemed to me at the time to be humorous; and I made my preparations with the most studious care. I took and furnished that house in Soho, to which Hyde was tracked by the police; and engaged as housekeeper a creature whom I well knew to be silent and unscrupulous. On the other side, I announced to my servants that a Mr. Hyde (whom I described) was to have full liberty and power about my house in the square; and to parry mishaps, I even called and made myself a familiar object, in my second character. I next drew up that will to which you so much objected; so that if anything befell me in the person of Dr. Jekyll, I could enter on that of Edward Hyde without pecuniary loss. And thus fortified, as I supposed, on every side, I began to profit by the strange immunities of my position.

Men have before hired bravos to transact their crimes, while their own person and reputation sat under shelter. I was the first that ever did so for his pleasures. I was the first that could thus plod in the public eye with a load of genial respectability, and in a moment, like a schoolboy, strip off these lendings and spring head-long into the sea of liberty. But for me, in my impenetrable mantle, the safety was complete. Think of it—I did not even exist! Let me but escape into my laboratory door, give me but a second or two to mix and swallow the draught that I had always standing ready; and

HENRY JEKYLL'S FULL STATEMENT OF THE CASE 65

whatever he had done, Edward Hyde would pass away like the stain of breath upon a mirror; and there in his stead, quietly at home, trimming the midnight lamp in his study, a man who could afford to laugh at suspicion, would be Henry Jekyll.

The pleasures which I made haste to seek in my disguise were, as I have said, undignified; I would scarce use a harder term. But in the hands of Edward Hyde, they soon began to turn towards the monstrous. When I would come back from these excursions, I was often plunged into a kind of wonder at my vicarious depravity. This familiar that I called out of my own soul, and sent forth alone to do his good pleasure, was a being inherently malign and villain-ous; his every act and thought centered on self; drinking pleasure with bestial avidity from any degree of torture to another; relent-less like a man of stone. Henry Jekyll stood at times aghast before the acts of Edward Hyde; but the situation was apart from ordin-ary laws, and insidiously relaxed the grasp of conscience. It was Hyde, after all, and Hyde alone, that was guilty. Jekyll was no worse; he woke again to his good qualities seemingly unimpaired; he would even make haste, where it was possible, to undo the evil done by Hyde. And thus his conscience slumbered.

Into the details of the infamy at which I thus connived (for even now I can scarce grant that I committed it) I have no design of entering; I mean but to point out the warnings and the success-ive steps with which my chastisement approached. I met with one accident which, as it brought on no consequence, I shall no more than mention. An act of cruelty to a child aroused against me the anger of a passer by, whom I recognised the other day in the person of your kinsman; the doctor and the child's family joined him; there were moments when I feared for my life; and at last, in order to pacify their too just resentment, Edward Hyde had to bring them to the door, and pay them in a cheque drawn in the name of Henry Jekyll. But this danger was easily eliminated from the future, by opening an account at another bank in the name of Edward Hyde himself; and when, by sloping my own hand back-ward, I had supplied my double with a signature, I thought I sat beyond the reach of fate.

Some two months before the murder of Sir Danvers, I had

been out for one of my adventures, had returned at a late hour, and woke the next day in bed with somewhat odd sensations. It was in vain I looked about me; in vain I saw the decent furniture and tall proportions of my room in the square; in vain that I recognised the pattern of the bed curtains and the design of the mahogany frame; something still kept insisting that I was not where I was, that I had not wakened where I seemed to be, but in the little room in Soho where I was accustomed to sleep in the body of Edward Hyde. I smiled to myself, and, in my psychological way, began lazily to inquire into the elements of this illusion, occasionally, even as I did so, dropping back into a comfortable morning doze. I was still so engaged when, in one of my more wakeful moments, my eye fell upon my hand. Now the hand of Henry Jekyll (as you have often remarked) was professional in shape and size: it was large, firm, white and comely. But the hand which I now saw, clearly enough, in the yellow light of a mid-London morning, lying half shut on the bed clothes, was lean, corded, knuckly, of a dusky pallor and thickly shaded with a swart growth of hair. It was the hand of Edward Hyde.

I must have stared upon it for near half a minute, sunk as I was in the mere stupidity of wonder, before terror woke up in my breast as sudden and startling as the crash of cymbals; and bounding from my bed, I rushed to the mirror. At the sight that met my eyes, my blood was changed into something exquisitely thin and icy. Yes, I had gone to bed Henry Jekyll, I had awakened Edward Hyde. How was this to be explained? I asked myself; and then, with another bound of terror—how was it to be remedied? It was well on in the morning; the servants were up; all my drugs were in the cabinet—a long journey down two pairs of stairs, through the back passage, across the open court and through the anatomical theatre, from where I was then standing horror-struck. It might indeed be possible to cover my face; but of what use was that, when I was unable to conceal the alteration in my stature? And then with an overpowering sweetness of relief, it came back upon my mind that the servants were already used to the coming and going of my second self. I had soon dressed, as well as I was able, in clothes of my own size: had soon passed through the house, where Bradshaw

HENRY JEKYLL'S FULL STATEMENT OF THE CASE   67

stared and drew back at seeing Mr. Hyde at such an hour and in such a strange array; and ten minutes later, Dr. Jekyll had returned to his own shape and was sitting down, with a darkened brow, to make a feint of breakfasting.

Small indeed was my appetite. This inexplicable incident, this reversal of my previous experience, seemed, like the Babylonian finger on the wall, to be spelling out the letters of my judgment; and I began to reflect more seriously than ever before on the issues and possibilities of my double existence. That part of me which I had the power of projecting, had lately been much exercised and nourished; it had seemed to me of late as though the body of Edward Hyde had grown in stature, as though (when I wore that form) I were conscious of a more generous tide of blood; and I began to spy a danger that, if this were much prolonged, the balance of my nature might be permanently overthrown, the power of voluntary change be forfeited, and the character of Edward Hyde become irrevocably mine. The power of the drug had not been always equally displayed. Once, very early in my career, it had totally failed me; since then I had been obliged on more than one occasion to double, and once, with infinite risk of death, to treble the amount; and these rare uncertainties had cast hitherto the sole shadow on my contentment. Now, however, and in the light of that morning's accident, I was led to remark that whereas, in the beginning, the difficulty had been to throw off the body of Jekyll, it had of late gradually but decidedly transferred itself to the other side. All things therefore seemed to point to this: that I was slowly losing hold of my original and better self, and becoming slowly incorporated with my second and worse.

Between these two, I now felt I had to choose. My two natures had memory in common, but all other faculties were most unequally shared between them. Jekyll (who was composite) now with the most sensitive apprehensions, now with a greedy gusto, projected and shared in the pleasures and adventures of Hyde; but Hyde was indifferent to Jekyll, or but remembered him as the mountain bandit remembers the cavern in which he conceals himself from pursuit. Jekyll had more than a father's interest; Hyde had more than a son's indifference. To cast in my lot with Jekyll, was to die to those appetites which I had long secretly indulged and had of late begun to pamper. To cast it in with Hyde, was to die to a thousand interests and aspirations, and to become, at a blow and forever, despised and friendless. The bargain might appear unequal; but there was still another consideration in the scales; for while Jekyll would suffer smartingly in the fires of abstinence, Hyde would be not even conscious of all that he had lost. Strange as my circumstances were, the terms of this debate are as old and commonplace as man; much the same inducements and alarms cast the die for any tempted and trembling sinner; and it fell out with me, as it falls with so vast a majority of my fellows, that I chose the better part and was found wanting in the strength to keep to it.

Yes, I preferred the elderly and discontented doctor, surrounded by friends and cherishing honest hopes; and bade a resolute farewell to the liberty, the comparative youth, the light step, leaping pulses and secret pleasures, that I had enjoyed in the disguise of Hyde. I made this choice perhaps with some unconscious reservation, for I neither gave up the house in Soho, nor destroyed the clothes of Edward Hyde, which still lay ready in my cabinet. For two months, however, I was true to my determination; for two months I led a life of such severity as I had never before attained to, and enjoyed the compensations of an approving conscience. But time began at last to obliterate the freshness of my alarm; the praises of conscience began to grow into a thing of course; I began to be tortured with throes and longings, as of Hyde struggling after freedom; and at last, in an hour of moral weakness, I once again compounded and swallowed the transforming draught.

I do not suppose that, when a drunkard reasons with himself upon his vice, he is once out of five hundred times affected by the dangers that he runs through his brutish, physical insensibility; neither had I, long as I had considered my position, made enough allowance for the complete moral insensibility and insensate readiness to evil, which were the leading characters of Edward Hyde. Yet it was by these that I was punished. My devil had been long caged, he came out roaring. I was conscious, even when I took the draught, of a more unbridled, a more furious propensity to ill. It must have been this, I suppose, that stirred in my soul that tempest of impatience with which I listened to the civilities of my unhappy victim; I declare at least, before God, no man morally sane could have been guilty of that crime upon so pitiful a provocation; and that I struck in no more reasonable spirit than that in which a sick child may break a plaything. But I had voluntarily stripped myself of all those balancing instincts, by which even the worst of us continues to walk with some degree of steadiness among temptations; and in my case, to be tempted, however slightly, was to fall.

Instantly the spirit of hell awoke in me and raged. With a transport of glee, I mauled the unresisting body, tasting delight from every blow; and it was not till weariness had begun to succeed, that I was suddenly, in the top fit of my delirium, struck through the heart by a cold thrill of terror. A mist dispersed; I saw my life to be forfeit; and fled from the scene of these excesses, at once glorying and trembling, my lust of evil gratified and stimulated, my love of life screwed to the topmost peg. I ran to the house in Soho, and (to make assurance doubly sure) destroyed my papers; thence I set out through the lamplit streets, in the same divided ecstasy of mind, gloating on my crime, light-headedly devising others in the future, and yet still hastening and still hearkening in my wake for the steps of the avenger. Hyde had a song upon his lips as he compounded the draught, and as he drank it, pledged the dead man. The pangs of transformation had not done tearing him, before Henry Jekyll, with streaming tears of gratitude and remorse, had fallen upon his knees and lifted his clasped hands to God. The veil of self-indulgence was rent from head to foot, I saw my life as a whole: I followed it up from the days of childhood, when I had walked with my father's hand, and through the self-denying toils of my professional life, to arrive again and again, with the same sense of unreality, at the damned horrors of the evening. I could have screamed aloud; I sought with tears and prayers to smother down the crowd of hideous images and sounds with which my memory swarmed against me; and still, between the petitions, the ugly face of my iniquity stared into my soul. As the acuteness of this remorse began to die away, it was succeeded by a sense of joy. The problem of my conduct was solved. Hyde was thenceforth impossible; whether I would or not, I was now confined to the better part of my existence; and O, how I rejoiced to think it! with what willing humility, I embraced anew the restrictions of natural life! with what sincere renunciation, I locked the door by which I had so often gone and come, and ground the key under my heel!

The next day, came the news that the murder had been over-looked, that the guilt of Hyde was patent to the world, and that the victim was a man high in public estimation. It was not only a crime, it had been a tragic folly. I think I was glad to know it; I think I was glad to have my better impulses thus buttressed and guarded by the terrors of the scaffold. Jekyll was now my city of refuge; let but Hyde peep out an instant, and the hands of all men would be raised to take and slay him.

I resolved in my future conduct to redeem the past; and I can say with honesty that my resolve was fruitful of some good. You know yourself how earnestly in the last months of last year, I laboured to relieve suffering; you know that much was done for others, and that the days passed quietly, almost happily for myself. Nor can I truly say that I wearied of this beneficent and innocent life; I think instead that I daily enjoyed it more completely; but I was still cursed with my duality of purpose; and as the first edge of my penitence wore off, the lower side of me, so long indulged, so recently chained down, began to growl for licence. Not that I dreamed of resuscitating Hyde; the bare idea of that would startle me to frenzy: no, it was in my own person, that I was once more tempted to trifle with my conscience; and it was as an ordinary secret sinner, that I at last fell before the assaults of temptation.

There comes an end to all things; the most capacious measure is filled at last; and this brief condescension to evil finally destroyed the balance of my soul. And yet I was not alarmed; the fall seemed natural, like a return to the old days before I had made my dis-covery. It was a fine, clear, January day, wet under foot where the frost had melted, but cloudless overhead; and the Regent's Park was full of winter chirrupings and sweet with Spring odours. I sat in the sun on a bench; the animal within me licking the chops of

HENRY JEKYLL'S FULL STATEMENT OF THE CASE 71

memory; the spiritual side a little drowsed, promising subsequent penitence, but not yet moved to begin. After all, I reflected, I was like my neighbours; and then I smiled, comparing myself with other men, comparing my active goodwill with the lazy cruelty of their neglect. And at the very moment of that vain glorious thought, a qualm came over me, a horrid nausea and the most deadly shuddering. These passed away, and left me faint; and then as in its turn the faintness subsided, I began to be aware of a change in the temper of my thoughts, a greater boldness, a contempt of danger, a solution of the bonds of obligation. I looked down; my clothes hung formlessly on my shrunken limbs; the hand that lay on my knee was corded and hairy. I was once more Edward Hyde. A moment before I had been safe of all men's respect, wealthy, beloved—the cloth laying for me in the dining room at home; and now I was the common quarry of mankind, hunted, houseless, a known murderer, thrall to the gallows.

My reason wavered, but it did not fail me utterly. I have more than once observed that, in my second character, my faculties seemed sharpened to a point and my spirits more tensely elastic; thus it came about that, where Jekyll perhaps might have succumbed, Hyde rose to the importance of the moment. My drugs were in one of the presses of my cabinet; how was I to reach them? That was the problem that (crushing my temples in my hands) I set myself to solve. The laboratory door I had closed. If I sought to enter by the house, my own servants would consign me to the gallows. I saw I must employ another hand, and thought of Lanyon. How was he to be reached? how persuaded? Supposing that I escaped capture in the streets, how was I to make my way into his presence? and how should I, an unknown and displeasing visitor, prevail on the famous physician to rifle the study of his colleague, Dr. Jekyll? Then I remembered that of my original character, one part remained to me: I could write my own hand; and once I had conceived that kindling spark, the way that I must follow became lighted up from end to end.

Thereupon, I arranged my clothes as best I could, and summoning a passing hansom, drove to an hotel in Portland Street, the name of which I chanced to remember. At my appearance (which was indeed comical enough, however tragic a fate these garments covered) the driver could not conceal his mirth. I gnashed my teeth upon him with a gust of devilish fury; and the smile withered from his face—happily for him—yet more happily for myself, for in another instant I had certainly dragged him from his perch. At the inn, as I entered, I looked about me with so black a countenance as made the attendants tremble; not a look did they exchange in my presence; but obsequiously took my orders, led me to a private room, and brought me wherewithal to write. Hyde in danger of his life was a creature new to me: shaken with inordinate anger, strung to the pitch of murder, lusting to inflict pain. Yet the creature was astute; mastered his fury with a great effort of the will; composed his two important letters, one to Lanyon and one to Poole; and that he might receive actual evidence of their being posted, sent them out with directions that they should be registered.

Thenceforward, he sat all day over the fire in the private room, gnawing his nails; there he dined, sitting alone with his fears, the waiter visibly quailing before his eye; and thence, when the night was fully come, he set forth in the corner of a closed cab, and was driven to and fro about the streets of the city. He, I say—I cannot say, I. That child of Hell had nothing human; nothing lived in him but fear and hatred. And when at last, thinking the driver had begun to grow suspicious, he discharged the cab and ventured on foot, attired in his misfitting clothes, an object marked out for observation, into the midst of the nocturnal passengers, these two base passions raged within him like a tempest. He walked fast, hunted by his fears, chattering to himself, skulking through the less frequented thoroughfares, counting the minutes that still divided him from midnight. Once a woman spoke to him, offering, I think, a box of lights. He smote her in the face, and she fled.

When I came to myself at Lanyon's, the horror of my old friend perhaps affected me somewhat: I do not know; it was at least but a drop in the sea to the abhorrence with which I looked back upon these hours. A change had come over me. It was no longer the fear of the gallows, it was the horror of being Hyde that racked me. I received Lanyon's condemnation partly in a dream; it was partly in a dream that I came home to my own house and got into bed. I slept after the prostration of the day, with a stringent and profound slumber which not even the nightmares that wrung me could avail to break. I awoke in the morning shaken, weakened, but refreshed. I still hated and feared the thought of the brute that slept within me, and I had not of course forgotten the appalling dangers of the day before; but I was once more at home, in my own house and close to my drugs; and gratitude for my escape shone so strong in my soul that it almost rivalled the brightness of hope.

I was stepping leisurely across the court after breakfast, drinking the chill of the air with pleasure, when I was seized again with those indescribable sensations that heralded the change; and I had but the time to gain the shelter of my cabinet, before I was once again raging and freezing with the passions of Hyde. It took on this occasion a double dose to recall me to myself; and alas! six hours after, as I sat looking sadly in the fire, the pangs returned, and the drug had to be re-administered. In short, from that day forth it seemed only by a great effort as of gymnastics, and only under the immediate stimulation of the drug, that I was able to wear the countenance of Jekyll. At all hours of the day and night, I would be taken with the premonitory shudder; above all, if I slept, or even dozed for a moment in my chair, it was always as Hyde that I awakened. Under the strain of this continually impending doom and by the sleeplessness to which I now condemned myself, ay, even beyond what I had thought possible to man, I became, in my own person, a creature eaten up and emptied by fever, languidly weak both in body and mind, and solely occupied by one thought: the horror of my other self. But when I slept, or when the virtue of the medicine wore off, I would leap almost without transition (for the pangs of transformation grew daily less marked) into the possession of a fancy brimming with images of terror, a soul boiling with causeless hatreds, and a body that seemed not strong enough to contain the raging energies of life. The powers of Hyde seemed to have grown with the sickliness of Jekyll. And certainly the hate that now divided them was equal on each side. With Jekyll, it was a thing of vital instinct. He had now seen the full deformity of that creature that shared with him some of the phenomena of consciousness, and was co-heir with him to death: and beyond these links of community, which in themselves made the most poignant part of his distress, he thought of Hyde, for all his energy of life, as of something not only hellish but inorganic. This was the shocking thing; that the slime of the pit seemed to utter cries and voices; that the amorphous dust gesticulated and sinned; that what was dead, and had no shape, should usurp the offices of life. And this again, that that insurgent horror was knit to him closer than a wife, closer than an eye; lay caged in his flesh, where he heard it mutter and felt it struggle to be born; and at every hour of weakness, and in the confidence of slumber, prevailed against him, and deposed him out of life. The hatred of Hyde for Jekyll, was of a different order. His terror of the gallows drove him continually to commit temporary suicide, and return to his subordinate station of a part instead of a person; but he loathed the necessity, he loathed the despondency into which Jekyll was now fallen, and he resented the dislike with which he was himself regarded. Hence the apelike tricks that he would play me, scrawling in my own hand blasphemies on the pages of my books, burning the letters and destroying the portrait of my father; and indeed, had it not been for his fear of death, he would long ago have ruined himself in order to involve me in the ruin. But his love of life is wonderful; I go further: I, who sicken and freeze at the mere thought of him, when I recall the abjection and passion of this attachment, and when I know how he fears my power to cut him off by suicide, I find it in my heart to pity him.

It is useless, and the time awfully fails me, to prolong this description; no one has ever suffered such torments, let that suffice; and yet even to these, habit brought—no, not alleviation— but a certain callousness of soul, a certain acquiescence of despair; and my punishment might have gone on for years, but for the last calamity which has now fallen, and which has finally severed me from my own face and nature. My provision of the salt, which had never been renewed since the date of the first experiment, began to run low. I sent out for a fresh supply, and mixed the draught; the ebullition followed, and the first change of colour, not the second; I drank it and it was without efficiency. You will learn from Poole

HENRY JEKYLL'S FULL STATEMENT OF THE CASE   75

how I have had London ransacked; it was in vain; and I am now persuaded that my first supply was impure, and that it was that unknown impurity which lent efficacy to the draught.

About a week has passed, and I am now finishing this statement under the influence of the last of the old powders. This, then, is the last time, short of a miracle, that Henry Jekyll can think his own thoughts or see his own face (now how sadly altered!) in the glass. Nor must I delay too long to bring my writing to an end; for if my narrative has hitherto escaped destruction, it has been by a combination of great prudence and great good luck. Should the throes of change take me in the act of writing it, Hyde will tear it in pieces; but if some time shall have elapsed after I have laid it by, his wonderful selfishness and circumscription to the moment will probably save it once again from the action of his apelike spite. And indeed the doom that is closing on us both, has already changed and crushed him. Half an hour from now, when I shall again and forever reindue that hated personality, I know how I shall sit shuddering and weeping in my chair, or continue, with the most strained and fear struck ecstasy of listening, to pace up and down this room (my last earthly refuge) and give ear to every sound of menace. Will Hyde die upon the scaffold? or will he find the courage to release himself at the last moment? God knows; I am careless; this is my true hour of death, and what is to follow concerns another than myself. Here then, as I lay down the pen and proceed to seal up my confession, I bring the life of that unhappy Henry Jekyll to an end.

Essays in the Art of Writing

LETTER TO A YOUNG GENTLEMAN
WHO PROPOSES TO EMBRACE THE CAREER OF ART

WITH the agreeable frankness of youth, you address me on a point of some practical importance to yourself and (it is even conceivable) of some gravity to the world: Should you or should you not become an artist? It is one which you must decide entirely for yourself; all that I can do is to bring under your notice some of the materials of that decision; and I will begin, as I shall probably conclude also, by assuring you that all depends on the vocation.

To know what you like is the beginning of wisdom and of old age. Youth is wholly experimental. The essence and charm of that unquiet and delightful epoch is ignorance of self as well as ignorance of life. These two unknowns the young man brings together again and again, now in the airiest touch, now with a bitter hug; now with exquisite pleasure, now with cutting pain; but never with indifference, to which he is a total stranger, and never with that near kinsman of indifference, contentment. If he be a youth of dainty senses or a brain easily heated, the interest of this series of experiments grows upon him out of all proportion to the pleasure he receives. It is not beauty that he loves, nor pleasure that he seeks, though he may think so; his design and his sufficient reward is to verify his own existence and taste the variety of human fate. To him, before the razor-edge of curiosity is dulled, all that is not actual living and the hot chase of experience wears a face of a disgusting dryness difficult to recall in later days; or if there be any exception—and here destiny steps in—it is in those moments when, wearied or surfeited of the primary activity of the senses, he calls up before memory the image of transacted pains and pleasures. Thus it is that such an one shies from all cut-and-dry professions, and inclines insensibly toward that career of art which consists only in the tasting and recording of experience.

This, which is not so much a vocation for art as an impatience of all other honest trades, frequently exists alone; and so existing, it will pass gently away in the course of years. Emphatically, it is not to be regarded, it is not a vocation, but a temptation; and when your father the other day so fiercely and (in my view) so properly discouraged your ambition, he was recalling not improbably some similar passage in his own experience. For the temptation is perhaps nearly as common as the vocation is rare. But again we have vocations which are imperfect; we have men whose minds are bound up, not so much in any art, as in the general *ars artium* and common base of all creative work; who will now dip into painting, and now study counterpoint, and anon will be inditing a sonnet: all these with equal interest, all often with genuine knowledge. And of this temper, when it stands alone, I find it difficult to speak; but I should counsel such an one to take to letters, for in literature (which drags with so wide a net) all his information may be found some day useful, and if he should go on as he has begun, and turn at last into the critic, he will have learned to use the necessary tools. Lastly we come to those vocations which are at once decisive and precise; to the men who are born with the love of pigments, the passion of drawing, the gift of music, or the impulse to create with words, just as other and perhaps the same men are born with the love of hunting, or the sea, or horses, or the turning-lathe. These are predestined; if a man love the labour of any trade apart from any question of success or fame, the gods have called him. He may have the general vocation too: he may have a taste for all the arts, and I think he often has; but the mark of his calling is this laborious partiality for one, this inextinguishable zest in its technical successes, and (perhaps above all) a certain candour of mind, to take his very trifling enterprise with a gravity that would befit the cares of empire, and to think the smallest improvement worth accomplishing at any expense of time and industry. The book, the statue, the sonata, must be gone upon with the unreasoning good faith and the unflagging spirit of children at their play. *Is it worth doing?*—when it shall have occurred to any

LETTER TO A YOUNG GENTLEMAN

artist to ask himself that question, it is implicitly answered in the negative. It does not occur to the child as he plays at being a pirate on the dining-room sofa, nor to the hunter as he pursues his quarry; and the candour of the one and the ardour of the other should be united in the bosom of the artist.

If you recognise in yourself some such decisive taste, there is no room for hesitation: follow your bent. And observe (lest I should too much discourage you) that the disposition does not usually burn so brightly at the first, or rather not so constantly. Habit and practice sharpen gifts; the necessity of toil grows less disgusting, grows even welcome in the course of years; a small taste (if it be only genuine) waxes with indulgence into an exclusive passion. Enough, just now, if you can look back over a fair interval, and see that your chosen art has a little more than held its own among the thronging interests of youth. Time will do the rest, if devotion help it; and soon your every thought will be engrossed in that beloved occupation.

But even with devotion, you may remind me, even with unfaltering and delighted industry, many thousand artists spend their lives, if the result be regarded, utterly in vain: a thousand artists, and never one work of art. But the vast mass of mankind are incapable of doing anything reasonably well, art among the rest. The worthless artist would not improbably have been a quite incompetent baker. And the artist, even if he does not amuse the public, amuses himself; so that there will always be one man the happier for his vigils. This is the practical side of art: its inexpugnable fortress for the true practitioner. The direct returns—the wages of the trade—are small, but the indirect—the wages of the life—are incalculably great. No other business offers a man his daily bread upon such joyful terms. The soldier and the explorer have moments of a worthier excitement, but they are purchased by cruel hardships and periods of tedium that beggar language. In the life of the artist there need be no hour without its pleasure. I take the author, with whose career I am best acquainted; and it is true he works in a rebellious material, and that the act of writing is cramped and trying both to the eyes and the temper; but remark him in his study, when matter crowds upon him and words are not wanting—in what a continual series of small successes time flows by; with what a sense of power as of one moving mountains, he marshals his petty characters; with what pleasures, both of the ear and eye, he sees his airy structure growing on the page; and how he labours in a craft to which the whole material of his life is tributary, and which opens a door to all his tastes, his loves, his hatreds, and his convictions, so that what he writes is only what he longed to utter. He may have enjoyed many things in this big, tragic playground of the world; but what shall he have enjoyed more fully than a morning of successful work? Suppose it ill paid: the wonder is it should be paid at all. Other men pay, and pay dearly, for pleasures less desirable.

Nor will the practice of art afford you pleasure only; it affords besides an admirable training. For the artist works entirely upon honour. The public knows little or nothing of those merits in the quest of which you are condemned to spend the bulk of your endeavours. Merits of design, the merit of first-hand energy, the merit of a certain cheap accomplishment which a man of the artistic temper easily acquires—these they can recognise, and these they value. But to those more exquisite refinements of proficiency and finish, which the artist so ardently desires and so keenly feels, for which (in the vigorous words of Balzac) he must toil "like a miner buried in a landslip," for which, day after day, he recasts and revises and rejects—the gross mass of the public must be ever blind. To those lost pains, suppose you attain the highest pitch of merit, posterity may possibly do justice; suppose, as is so probable, you fail by even a hair's breadth of the highest, rest certain they shall never be observed. Under the shadow of this cold thought, alone in his studio, the artist must preserve from day to day his constancy to the ideal. It is this which makes his life noble; it is by this that the practice of his craft strengthens and matures his character; it is for this that even the serious countenance of the great emperor was turned approvingly (if only for a moment) on the followers of Apollo, and that sternly gentle voice bade the artist cherish his art.

And here there fall two warnings to be made. First, if you are to continue to be a law to yourself, you must beware of the first signs

LETTER TO A YOUNG GENTLEMAN 83

of laziness. This idealism in honesty can only be supported by
perpetual effort; the standard is easily lowered, the artist who says
"*It will do*," is on the downward path; three or four pot-boilers are
enough at times (above all at wrong times) to falsify a talent, and
by the practice of journalism a man runs the risk of becoming
wedded to cheap finish. This is the danger on the one side; there
is not less upon the other. The consciousness of how much the
artist is (and must be) a law to himself, debauches the small
heads. Perceiving recondite merits very hard to attain, making or
swallowing artistic formulæ, or perhaps falling in love with some
particular proficiency of his own, many artists forget the end of all
art: to please. It is doubtless tempting to exclaim against the
ignorant bourgeois; yet it should not be forgotten, it is he who is to
pay us, and that (surely on the face of it) for services that he shall
desire to have performed. Here also, if properly considered, there
is a question of transcendental honesty. To give the public what
they do not want, and yet expect to be supported: we have there
a strange pretension, and yet not uncommon, above all with
painters. The first duty in this world is for a man to pay his way;
when that is quite accomplished, he may plunge into what
eccentricity he likes; but emphatically not till then. Till then, he
must pay assiduous court to the bourgeois who carries the purse.
And if in the course of these capitulations he shall falsify his talent,
it can never have been a strong one, and he will have preserved a
better thing than talent—character. Or if he be of a mind so
independent that he cannot stoop to this necessity, one course is
yet open: he can desist from art, and follow some more manly way
of life.

I speak of a more manly way of life, it is a point on which
I must be frank. To live by a pleasure is not a high calling; it
involves patronage, however veiled; it numbers the artist, however
ambitious, along with dancing-girls and billiard-markers. The
French have a romantic evasion for one employment, and call its
practitioners the Daughters of Joy. The artist is of the same family,
he is of the Sons of Joy, chose his trade to please himself, gains
his livelihood by pleasing others, and has parted with something
of the sterner dignity of man. Journals but a little while ago

declaimed against the Tennyson peerage; and this Son of Joy was blamed for condescension when he followed the example of Lord Lawrence and Lord Cairns and Lord Clyde. The poet was more happily inspired; with a better modesty he accepted the honour; and anonymous journalists have not yet (if I am to believe them) recovered the vicarious disgrace to their profession. When it comes to their turn, these gentlemen can do themselves more justice; and I shall be glad to think of it; for to my barbarian eyesight, even Lord Tennyson looks somewhat out of place in that assembly. There should be no honours for the artist; he has already, in the practice of his art, more than his share of the rewards of life; the honours are pre-empted for other trades, less agreeable and perhaps more useful.

But the devil in these trades of pleasing is to fail to please. In ordinary occupations, a man offers to do a certain thing or to produce a certain article with a merely conventional accomplishment, a design in which (we may almost say) it is difficult to fail. But the artist steps forth out of the crowd and proposes to delight: an impudent design, in which it is impossible to fail without odious circumstances. The poor Daughter of Joy, carrying her smiles and finery quite unregarded through the crowd, makes a figure which it is impossible to recall without a wounding pity. She is the type of the unsuccessful artist. The actor, the dancer, and the singer must appear like her in person, and drain publicly the cup of failure. But though the rest of us escape this crowning bitterness of the pillory, we all court in essence the same humiliation. We all profess to be able to delight. And how few of us are! We all pledge ourselves to be able to continue to delight. And the day will come to each, and even to the most admired, when the ardour shall have declined and the cunning shall be lost, and he shall sit by his deserted booth ashamed. Then shall he see himself condemned to do work for which he blushes to take payment. Then (as if his lot were not already cruel) he must lie exposed to the gibes of the wreckers of the press, who earn a little bitter bread by the condemnation of trash which they have not read, and the praise of excellence which they cannot understand.

And observe that this seems almost the necessary end at least of

LETTER TO A YOUNG GENTLEMAN   85

writers. *Les Blancs et les Bleus* (for instance) is of an order of merit
very different from *Le Vicomte de Bragelonne*; and if any gentleman
can bear to spy upon the nakedness of *Castle Dangerous*, his name
I think is Ham: let it be enough for the rest of us to read of it (not
without tears) in the pages of Lockhart. Thus in old age, when
occupation and comfort are most needful, the writer must lay
aside at once his pastime and his breadwinner. The painter indeed,
if he succeed at all in engaging the attention of the public, gains
great sums and can stand to his easel until a great age without
dishonourable failure. The writer has the double misfortune to be
ill-paid while he can work, and to be incapable of working when he
is old. It is thus a way of life which conducts directly to a false
position.

For the writer (in spite of notorious examples to the contrary)
must look to be ill-paid. Tennyson and Montépin make handsome
livelihoods; but we cannot all hope to be Tennyson, and we do not
all perhaps desire to be Montépin. If you adopt an art to be your
trade, weed your mind at the outset of all desire of money.
What you may decently expect, if you have some talent and much
industry, is such an income as a clerk will earn with a tenth or
perhaps a twentieth of your nervous output. Nor have you the
right to look for more; in the wages of the life, not in the wages of
the trade, lies your reward; the work is here the wages. It will be
seen I have little sympathy with the common lamentations of the
artist class. Perhaps they do not remember the hire of the field
labourer; or do they think no parallel will lie? Perhaps they have
never observed what is the retiring allowance of a field officer; or
do they suppose their contributions to the arts of pleasing more
important than the services of a colonel? Perhaps they forget on
how little Millet was content to live; or do they think, because they
have less genius, they stand excused from the display of equal
virtues? But upon one point there should be no dubiety: if a man
be not frugal, he has no business in the arts. If he be not frugal, he
steers directly for that last tragic scene of *le vieux saltimbanque*;
if he be not frugal, he will find it hard to continue to be honest.
Some day, when the butcher is knocking at the door, he may be
tempted, he may be obliged, to turn out and sell a slovenly piece of

work. If the obligation shall have arisen through no wantonness of his own, he is even to be commanded; for words cannot describe how far more necessary it is that a man should support his family, than that he should attain to—or preserve—distinction in the arts. But if the pressure comes through his own fault, he has stolen, and stolen under trust, and stolen (which is the worst of all) in such a way that no law can reach him.

And now you may perhaps ask me, if the debutant artist is to have no thought of money, and if (as is implied) he is to expect no honours from the State, he may not at least look forward to the delights of popularity? Praise, you will tell me, is a savoury dish. And in so far as you may mean the countenance of other artists, you would put your finger on one of the most essential and enduring pleasures of the career of art. But in so far as you should have an eye to the commendations of the public or the notice of the newspapers, be sure you would but be cherishing a dream. It is true that in certain esoteric journals the author (for instance) is duly criticised, and that he is often praised a great deal more than he deserves, sometimes for qualities which he prided himself on eschewing, and sometimes by ladies and gentlemen who have denied themselves the privilege of reading his work. But if a man be sensitive to this wild praise, we must suppose him equally alive to that which often accompanies and always follows it—wild ridicule. A man may have done well for years, and then he may fail; he will hear of his failure. Or he may have done well for years, and still do well, but the critics may have tired of praising him, or there may have sprung up some new idol of the instant, some "dust a little gilt," to whom they now prefer to offer sacrifice. Here is the obverse and the reverse of that empty and ugly thing called popularity. Will any man suppose it worth the gaining?

BOOKS WHICH HAVE INFLUENCED ME

~~~~~~

THE EDITOR has somewhat insidiously laid a trap for his corres-
pondents, the question put appearing at first so innocent, truly
cutting so deep. It is not, indeed, until after some reconnaissance
and review that the writer awakes to find himself engaged upon
something in the nature of autobiography, or, perhaps worse,
upon a chapter in the life of that little, beautiful brother whom we
once all had, and whom we have all lost and mourned, the man we
ought to have been, the man we hoped to be. But when word has
been passed (even to an editor), it should, if possible, be kept; and
if sometimes I am wise and say too little, and sometimes weak and
say too much, the blame must lie at the door of the person who
entrapped me.

The most influential books, and the truest in their influence,
are works of fiction. They do not pin the reader to a dogma which
he must afterwards discover to be inexact; they do not teach him
a lesson which he must afterwards unlearn. They repeat, they
rearrange, they clarify the lessons of life; they disengage us from
ourselves, they constrain us to the acquaintance of others; and they
show us the web of experience, not as we can see it for ourselves,
but with a singular change—that monstrous, consuming *ego* of
ours being, for the nonce, struck out. To be so, they must be
reasonably true to the human comedy; and any work that is so
serves the turn of instruction. But the course of our education is
answered best by those poems and romances where we breathe a
magnanimous atmosphere of thought and meet generous and
pious characters. Shakespeare has served me best. Few living
friends have had upon me an influence so strong for good as
Hamlet or Rosalind. The last character, already well beloved in

88   ESSAYS IN THE ART OF WRITING

the reading, I had the good fortune to see, I must think, in an impressionable hour, played by Mrs. Scott Siddons. Nothing has ever more moved, more delighted, more refreshed me; nor has the influence quite passed away. Kent's brief speech over the dying Lear had a great effect upon my mind, and was the burthen of my reflections for long, so profoundly, so touchingly generous did it appear in sense, so overpowering in expression. Perhaps my dearest and best friend outside of Shakespeare is D'Artagnan—the elderly D'Artagnan of the *Vicomte de Bragelonne*. I know not a more human soul, nor, in his way, a finer; I shall be very sorry for the man who is so much of a pedant in morals that he cannot learn from the Captain of Musketeers. Lastly, I must name the *Pilgrim's Progress*, a book that breathes of every beautiful and valuable emotion.

But of works of art little can be said; their influence is profound and silent, like the influence of nature; they mould by contact; we drink them up like water, and are bettered, yet know not how. It is in books more specifically didactic that we can follow out the effect, and distinguish and weigh and compare. A book which has been very influential upon me fell early into my hands, and so may stand first, though I think its influence was only sensible later on, and perhaps still keeps growing, for it is a book not easily outlived; the *Essais* of Montaigne. That temperate and genial picture of life is a great gift to place in the hands of persons of to-day; they will find in these smiling pages a magazine of heroism and wisdom, all of an antique strain; they will have their "linen decencies" and excited orthodoxies fluttered, and will (if they have any gift of reading) perceive that these have not been fluttered without some excuse and ground of reason; and (again if they have any gift of reading) they will end by seeing that this old gentleman was in a dozen ways a finer fellow, and held in a dozen ways a nobler view of life than they or their contemporaries.

The next book, in order of time, to influence me, was the New Testament, and in particular the Gospel according to St. Matthew. I believe it would startle and move any one if they could make a certain effort of imagination and read it freshly like a book, not droningly and dully like a portion of the Bible. Any one would

BOOKS WHICH HAVE INFLUENCED ME 89

then be able to see in it those truths which we are all courteously supposed to know and all modestly refrain from applying. But upon this subject it is perhaps better to be silent.

I come next to Whitman's *Leaves of Grass*, a book of singular service, a book which tumbled the world upside down for me, blew into space a thousand cobwebs of genteel and ethical illusion, and, having thus shaken my tabernacle of lies, set me back again upon a strong foundation of all the original and manly virtues. But it is, once more, only a book for those who have the gift of reading. I will be very frank—I believe it is so with all good books except, perhaps, fiction. The average man lives, and must live, so wholly in convention, that gunpowder charges of the truth are more apt to discompose than to invigorate his creed. Either he cries out upon blasphemy and indecency, and crouches the closer round that little idol of part-truths and part-conveniences which is the contemporary deity, or he is convinced by what is new, forgets what is old, and becomes truly blasphemous and indecent himself. New truth is only useful to supplement the old; rough truth is only wanted to expand, not to destroy, our civil and often elegant conventions. He who cannot judge had better stick to fiction and the daily papers. There he will get little harm, and, in the first at least, some good.

Close upon the back of my discovery of Whitman, I came under the influence of Herbert Spencer. No more persuasive rabbi exists, and few better. How much of his vast structure will bear the touch of time, how much is clay and how much brass, it were too curious to inquire. But his words, if dry, are always manly and honest; there dwells in his pages a spirit of highly abstract joy, plucked naked like an algebraic symbol but still joyful; and the reader will find there a *caput-mortuum* of piety, with little indeed of its loveliness, but with most of its essentials; and these two qualities make him a wholesome, as his intellectual vigour makes him a bracing, writer. I should be much of a hound if I lost my gratitude to Herbert Spencer.

Goethe's Life, by Lewes, had a great importance for me when it first fell into my hands—a strange instance of the partiality of man's good and man's evil. I know no one whom I less admire than

Goethe; he seems a very epitome of the sins of genius, breaking open the doors of private life and wantonly wounding friends, in that crowning offence of *Werther*, and in his own character a mere pen-and-ink Napoleon, conscious of the rights and duties of superior talents as a Spanish inquisitor was conscious of the rights and duties of his office. And yet in his fine devotion to his art, in his honest and serviceable friendship for Schiller, what lessons are contained! Biography, usually so false to its office, does here for once perform for us some of the work of fiction, reminding us, that is, of the truly mingled tissue of man's nature, and how huge faults and shining virtues cohabit and persevere in the same character. History serves us well to this effect, but in the originals not in the pages of the popular epitomiser, who is bound, by the very nature of his task, to make us feel the difference of epochs instead of the essential identity of man, and even in the originals only to those who can recognise their own human virtues and defects in strange forms often inverted, and under strange names often interchanged. Martial is a poet of no good repute and it gives a man new thoughts to read his works dispassionately, and find in this unseemly jester's serious passages the image of a kind, wise, and self-respecting gentleman. It is customary, I suppose, in reading Martial, to leave out these pleasant verses; I never heard of them, at least, until I found them for myself; and this partiality is one among a thousand things that help to build up our distorted and hysterical conception of the great Roman Empire.

This brings us by a natural transition to a very noble book—the *Meditations* of Marcus Aurelius. The dispassionate gravity, the noble forgetfulness of self, the tenderness of others, that are there expressed and were practised on so great a scale in the life of its writer, make this book a book quite by itself. No one can read it and not be moved. Yet it scarcely or rarely appeals to the feelings—those very mobile, those not very trusty parts of man. Its address lies further back: its lesson comes more deeply home; when you have read, you carry away with you a memory of the man himself; it is as though you had touched a loyal hand, looked into brave eyes, and made a noble friend; there is another bond on you

BOOKS WHICH HAVE INFLUENCED ME   91

thenceforward, binding you to life and to the love of virtue.

Wordsworth should perhaps come next. Every one has been influenced by Wordsworth, and it is hard to tell precisely how. A certain innocence, a rugged austerity of joy, a sight of the stars, "the silence that is in the lonely hills," something of the cold thrill of dawn, cling to his work and give it a particular address to what is best in us. I do not know that you learn a lesson; you need not—Mill did not—agree with any one of his beliefs; and yet the spell is cast. Such are the best teachers: a dogma learned is only a new error—the old one was perhaps as good; but a spirit communicated is a perpetual possession. These best teachers climb beyond teaching to the plane of art; it is themselves, and what is best in themselves, that they communicate.

I should never forgive myself if I forgot *The Egoist*. It is art, if you like, but it belongs purely to didactic art, and from all the novels I have read (and I have read thousands) stands in a place by itself. Here is a Nathan for the modern David; here is a book to send the blood into men's faces. Satire, the angry picture of human faults, is not great art; we can all be angry with our neighbour; what we want is to be shown, not his defects, of which we are too conscious, but his merits, to which we are too blind. And *The Egoist* is a satire; so much must be allowed; but it is a satire of a singular quality, which tells you nothing of that obvious mote, which is engaged from first to last with that invisible beam. It is yourself that is hunted down; these are your own faults that are dragged into the day and numbered, with lingering relish, with cruel cunning and precision. A young friend of Mr. Meredith's (as I have the story) came to him in an agony. "This is too bad of you," he cried. "Willoughby is me!" "No, my dear fellow," said the author; "he is all of us." I have read *The Egoist* five or six times myself, and I mean to read it again; for I am like the young friend of the anecdote—I think Willoughby an unmanly but a very serviceable exposure of myself.

I suppose, when I am done, I shall find that I have forgotten much that was most influential, as I see already I have forgotten Thoreau, and Hazlitt whose paper "On the Spirit of Obligations" was a turning-point in my life, and Penn whose little book of aphorisms had a brief but strong effect on me, and Mitford's *Tales of Old Japan*, wherein I learned for the first time the proper attitude of any rational man to his country's laws—a secret found, and kept, in the Asiatic islands. That I should commemorate all is more than I can hope or the Editor could ask. It will be more to the point, after having said so much upon improving books, to say a word or two about the improvable reader. The gift of reading, as I have called it, is not very common, nor very generally understood. It consists, first of all, in a vast intellectual endowment—a free grace, I find I must call it—by which a man rises to understand that he is not punctually right, nor those from whom he differs absolutely wrong. He may hold dogmas; he may hold them passionately; and he may know that others hold them but coldly, or hold them differently, or hold them not at all. Well, if he has the gift of reading, these others will be full of meat for him. They will see the other side of propositions and the other side of virtues. He need not change his dogma for that, but he may change his reading of that dogma, and he must supplement and correct his deductions from it. A human truth, which is always very much a lie, hides as much of life as it displays. It is men who hold another truth, or, as it seems to us, perhaps, a dangerous lie, who can extend our restricted field of knowledge, and rouse our drowsy consciences. Something that seems quite new, or that seems insolently false or very dangerous, is the test of a reader. If he tries to see what it means, what truth excuses it, he has the gift, and let him read. If he is merely hurt, or offended, or exclaims upon his author's folly, he had better take to the daily papers; he will never be a reader.

And here, with the aptest illustrative force, after I have laid down my part-truth, I must step in with its opposite. For, after all, we are vessels of a very limited content. Not all men can read all books; it is only in a chosen few that any man will find his appointed food; and the fittest lessons are the most palatable, and make themselves welcome to the mind. A writer learns this early, and it is his chief support; he goes on unafraid, laying down the law; and he is sure at heart that most of what he says is demonstrably false, and much of a mingled strain, and some

BOOKS WHICH HAVE INFLUENCED ME

hurtful, and very little good for service; but he is sure besides that when his words fall into the hands of any genuine reader, they will be weighed and winnowed, and only that which suits will be assimilated; and when they fall into the hands of one who cannot intelligently read, they come there quite silent and inarticulate, falling upon deaf ears, and his secret is kept as if he had not written.

A NOTE ON REALISM

STYLE is the invariable mark of any master; and for the student who does not aspire so high as to be numbered with the giants, it is still the one quality in which he may improve himself at will. Passion, wisdom, creative force, the power of mystery or colour, are allotted in the hour of birth, and can be neither learned nor simulated. But the just and dexterous use of what qualities we have, the proportion of one part to another and to the whole, the elision of the useless, the accentuation of the important, and the preservation of a uniform character from end to end—these, which taken together constitute technical perfection, are to some degree within the reach of industry and intellectual courage. What to put in and what to leave out; whether some particular fact be organically necessary or purely ornamental; whether, if it be purely ornamental, it may not weaken or obscure the general design; and finally, whether, if we decide to use it, we should do so grossly and notably or in some conventional disguise: are questions of plastic style continually re-arising. And the sphinx that patrols the highways of executive art has no more unanswerable riddle to propound.

In literature (from which I must draw my instances) the great change of the past century has been effected by the admission of detail. It was inaugurated by the romantic Scott; and at length, by the semi-romantic Balzac and his more or less wholly unromantic followers, bound like a duty on the novelist. For some time it signified and expressed a more ample contemplation of the conditions of man's life; but it has recently (at least in France) fallen into a merely technical and decorative stage, which it is, perhaps, still too harsh to call survival. With a movement of alarm,

A NOTE ON REALISM

the wiser or more timid begin to fall a little back from these extremities; they begin to aspire after a more naked, narrative articulation; after the succinct, the dignified, and the poetic; and as a means to this, after a general lightening of this baggage of detail. After Scott we beheld the starveling story—once, in the hands of Voltaire, as abstract as a parable—begin to be pampered upon facts. The introduction of these details developed a particular ability of hand; and that ability, childishly indulged, has led to the works that now amaze us on a railway journey. A man of the unquestionable force of M. Zola spends himself on technical successes. To afford a popular flavour and attract the mob, he adds a steady current of what I may be allowed to call the rancid. That is exciting to the moralist; but what more particularly interests the artist is this tendency of the extreme of detail, when followed as a principle, to degenerate into mere *feux-de-joie* of literary tricking. The other day even M. Daudet was to be heard babbling of audible colours and visible sounds.

This odd suicide of one branch of the realists may serve to remind us of the fact which underlies a very dusty conflict of the critics. All representative art, which can be said to live, is both realistic and ideal; and the realism about which we quarrel is a matter purely of externals. It is no especial cultus of nature and veracity, but a mere whim of veering fashion, that has made us turn our back upon the larger, more various, and more romantic art of yore. A photographic exactitude in dialogue is now the exclusive fashion; but even in the ablest hands it tells us no more— I think it even tells us less—than Molière, wielding his artificial medium, has told to us and to all time of Alceste or Orgon, Dorine or Chrysale. The historical novel is forgotten. Yet truth to the conditions of man's nature and the conditions of man's life, the truth of literary art, is free of the ages. It may be told us in a carpet comedy, in a novel of adventure, or a fairy tale. The scene may be pitched in London, on the sea-coast of Bohemia, or away on the mountains of Beulah. And by an odd and luminous accident, if there is any page of literature calculated to awake the envy of M. Zola, it must be that *Troilus and Cressida* which Shakespeare, in a spasm of unmanly anger with the world, grafted on the heroic story of the siege of Troy.

This question of realism, let it then be clearly understood, regards not in the least degree the fundamental truth, but only the technical method, of a work of art. Be as ideal or as abstract as you please, you will be none the less veracious; but if you be weak, you run the risk of being tedious and inexpressive; and if you be very strong and honest, you may chance upon a masterpiece.

A work of art is first cloudily conceived in the mind; during the period of gestation it stands more clearly forward from these swaddling mists, puts on expressive lineaments, and becomes at length that most faultless, but also, alas! that incommunicable product of the human mind, a perfected design. On the approach to execution all is changed. The artist must now step down, don his working clothes, and become the artisan. He now resolutely commits his airy conception, his delicate Ariel, to the touch of matter; he must decide, almost in a breath, the scale, the style, the spirit, and the particularity of execution of his whole design.

The engendering idea of some works is stylistic; a technical preoccupation stands them instead of some robuster principle of life. And with these the execution is but play; for the stylistic problem is resolved beforehand, and all large originality of treatment wilfully foregone. Such are the verses, intricately designed, which we have learnt to admire, with a certain smiling admiration, at the hands of Mr. Lang and Mr. Dobson; such, too, are those canvases where dexterity or even breadth of plastic style takes the place of pictorial nobility of design. So, it may be remarked, it was easier to begin to write *Esmond* than *Vanity Fair*, since, in the first, the style was dictated by the nature of the plan; and Thackeray, a man probably of some indolence of mind, enjoyed and got good profit of this economy of effort. But the case is exceptional. Usually in all works of art that have been conceived from within outwards, and generously nourished from the author's mind, the moment in which he begins to execute is one of extreme perplexity and strain. Artists of indifferent energy and an imperfect devotion to their own ideal make this ungrateful effort once for all; and, having formed a style, adhere to it through life. But those of a higher order cannot rest content with a process

A NOTE ON REALISM

which, as they continue to employ it, must infallibly degenerate toward the academic and the cut-and-dried. Every fresh work in which they embark is the signal for a fresh engagement of the whole forces of their mind; and the changing views which accompany the growth of their experience are marked by still more sweeping alterations in the manner of their art. So that criticism loves to dwell upon and distinguish the varying periods of a Raphael, a Shakespeare, or a Beethoven.

It is, then, first of all, at this initial and decisive moment when execution is begun, and thenceforth only in a less degree, that the ideal and the real do indeed, like good and evil angels, contend for the direction of the work. Marble, paint, and language, the pen, the needle, and the brush, all have their grossnesses, their ineffable impotences, their hours, if I may so express myself, of insubordination. It is the work and it is a great part of the delight of any artist to contend with these unruly tools, and now by brute energy, now by witty expedient, to drive and coax them to effect his will. Given these means, so laughably inadequate, and given the interest, the intensity, and the multiplicity of the actual sensation whose effect he is to render with their aid, the artist has one main and necessary resource which he must, in every case and upon any theory, employ. He must, that is, suppress much and omit more. He must omit what is tedious or irrelevant, and suppress what is tedious and necessary. But such facts as, in regard to the main design, subserve a variety of purposes, he will perforce and eagerly retain. And it is the mark of the very highest order of creative art to be woven exclusively of such. There, any fact that is registered is contrived a double or a treble debt to pay, and is at once an ornament in its place and a pillar in the main design. Nothing would find room in such a picture that did not serve, at once, to complete the composition, to accentuate the scheme of colour, to distinguish the planes of distance, and to strike the note of the selected sentiment; nothing would be allowed in such a story that did not, at the same time, expedite the progress of the fable, build up the characters, and strike home the moral or the philosophical design. But this is unattainable. As a rule, so far from building the fabric of our works exclusively with these, we are thrown into a rapture if we think we can muster a dozen or a score of them, to be the plums of our confection. And hence, in order that the canvas may be filled or the story proceed from point to point, other details must be admitted. They must be admitted, alas! upon a doubtful title; many without marriage robes. Thus any work of art, as it proceeds toward completion, too often—I had almost written always—loses in force and poignancy of main design. Our little air is swamped and dwarfed among hardly relevant orchestration; our little passionate story drowns in a deep sea of descriptive eloquence or slipshod talk.

But again, we are rather more tempted to admit those particulars which we know we can describe; and hence those most of all which, having been described very often, have grown to be conventionally treated in the practice of our art. These we choose, as the mason chooses the acanthus to adorn his capital, because they come naturally to the accustomed hand. The old stock incidents and accessories, tricks of workmanship and schemes of composition (all being admirably good, or they would long have been forgotten) haunt and tempt our fancy, offer us ready-made but not perfectly appropriate solutions for any problem that arises, and wean us from the study of nature and the uncompromising practice of art. To struggle, to face nature, to find fresh solutions, and give expression to facts which have not yet been adequately or not yet elegantly expressed, is to run a little upon the danger of extreme self-love. Difficulty sets a high price upon achievement; and the artist may easily fall into the error of the French naturalists, and consider any fact as welcome to admission if it be the ground of brilliant handiwork; or, again, into the error of the modern landscape-painter, who is apt to think that difficulty overcome and science well displayed can take the place of what is, after all, the one excuse and breath of art— charm. A little further, and he will regard charm in the light of an unworthy sacrifice to prettiness, and the omission of a tedious passage as an infidelity to art.

We have now the matter of this difference before us. The idealist, his eye singly fixed upon the greater outlines, loves rather to fill up the interval with detail of the conventional order, briefly touched, soberly suppressed in tone, courting neglect. But the realist, with a fine intemperance, will not suffer the presence of anything so dead as a convention; he shall have all fiery, all hot-pressed from nature, all charactered and notable, seizing the eye. The style that befits either of these extremes, once chosen, brings with it its necessary disabilities and dangers. The immediate danger of the realist is to sacrifice the beauty and significance of the whole to local dexterity, or, in the insane pursuit of completion, to immolate his readers under facts; but he comes in the last resort, and as his energy declines, to discard all design, abjure all choice, and, with scientific thoroughness, steadily to communicate matter which is not worth learning. The danger of the idealist is, of course, to become merely null and lose all grip of fact, particularity, or passion.

We talk of bad and good. Everything, indeed, is good which is conceived with honesty and executed with communicative ardour. But though on neither side is dogmatism fitting, and though in every case the artist must decide for himself, and decide afresh and yet afresh for each succeeding work and new creation; yet one thing may be generally said, that we of the last quarter of the nineteenth century, breathing as we do the intellectual atmosphere of our age, are more apt to err upon the side of realism than to sin in quest of the ideal. Upon that theory it may be well to watch and correct our own decisions, always holding back the hand from the least appearance of irrelevant dexterity, and resolutely fixed to begin no work that is not philosophical, passionate, dignified, happily mirthful, or, at the last and least, romantic in design.

THE MORALITY OF THE PROFESSION OF LETTERS

THE profession of letters has been lately debated in the public prints; and it has been debated, to put the matter mildly, from a point of view that was calculated to surprise high-minded men, and bring a general contempt on books and reading. Some time ago, in particular, a lively, pleasant, popular writer devoted an essay, lively and pleasant like himself, to a very encouraging view of the profession. We may be glad that his experience is so cheering, and we may hope that all others, who deserve it, shall be as handsomely rewarded; but I do not think we need be at all glad to have this question, so important to the public and ourselves, debated solely on the ground of money. The salary in any business under heaven is not the only, nor indeed the first, question. That you should continue to exist is a matter for your own consideration; but that your business should be first honest, and second useful, are points in which honour and morality are concerned. If the writer to whom I refer succeeds in persuading a number of young persons to adopt this way of life with an eye set singly on the livelihood, we must expect them in their works to follow profit only, and we must expect in consequence, if he will pardon me the epithets, a slovenly, base, untrue, and empty literature. Of that writer himself I am not speaking: he is diligent, clean and pleasing; we all owe him periods of entertainment, and he has achieved an amiable popularity which he has adequately deserved. But the truth is, he does not, or did not when he first embraced it, regard his profession from this purely mercenary side. He went into it, I shall venture to say, if not with any noble design, at least in the ardour of a first love; and he enjoyed its practice long before he paused to calculate the wage. The other day an author was

THE MORALITY OF THE PROFESSION OF LETTERS 101

complimented on a piece of work, good in itself and exceptionally good for him, and replied, in terms unworthy of a commercial traveller, that as the book was not briskly selling he did not give a copper farthing for its merit. It must not be supposed that the person to whom this answer was addressed received it as a profession of faith; he knew, on the other hand, that it was only a whiff of irritation; just as we know, when a respectable writer talks of literature as a way of life, like shoemaking, but not so useful, that he is only debating one aspect of a question, and is still clearly conscious of a dozen others more important in themselves and more central to the matter in hand. But while those who treat literature in this penny-wise and virtue-foolish spirit are themselves truly in possession of a better light, it does not follow that the treatment is decent or improving, whether for themselves or others. To treat all subjects in the highest, the most honourable, and the pluckiest spirit, consistent with the fact, is the first duty of a writer. If he be well paid, as I am glad to hear he is, this duty becomes the more urgent, the neglect of it the more disgraceful. And perhaps there is no subject on which a man should speak so gravely as that industry, whatever it may be, which is the occupation or delight of his life; which is his tool to earn or serve with; and which, if it be unworthy, stamps himself as a mere incubus of dumb and greedy bowels on the shoulders of labouring humanity. On that subject alone even to force the note might lean to virtue's side. It is to be hoped that a numerous and enterprising generation of writers will follow and surpass the present one; but it would be better if the stream were stayed, and the roll of our old honest English books were closed, than that esurient book-makers should continue and debase a brave tradition, and lower, in their own eyes, a famous race. Better that our serene temples were deserted than filled with trafficking and juggling priests.

There are two just reasons for the choice of any way of life: the first is inbred taste in the chooser; the second some high utility in the industry selected. Literature, like any other art, is singularly interesting to the artist; and, in a degree peculiar to itself among the arts, it is useful to mankind. These are sufficient justifications for any young man or woman who adopts it as the business of his life. I shall not say much about the wages. A writer can live by his writing. If not so luxuriously as by other trades, then less luxuriously. The nature of the work he does all day will more affect his happiness than the quality of his dinner at night. Whatever be your calling and however much it brings you in the year, you could still, you know, get more by cheating. We all suffer ourselves to be too much concerned about a little poverty; but such considerations should not move us in the choice of that which is to be the business and justification of so great a portion of our lives; and like the missionary, the patriot, or the philosopher, we should all choose that poor and brave career in which we can do the most and best for mankind. Now Nature, faithfully followed, proves herself a careful mother. A lad, for some liking to the jingle of words, betakes himself to letters for his life; by-and-by, when he learns more gravity, he finds that he has chosen better than he knew; that if he earns little, he is earning it amply; that if he receives a small wage, he is in a position to do considerable services; that it is in his power, in some small measure to protect the oppressed and to defend the truth. So kindly is the world arranged, such great profit may arise from a small degree of human reliance on oneself, and such, in particular, is the happy star of this trade of writing, that it should combine pleasure and profit to both parties, and be at once agreeable, like fiddling, and useful, like good preaching.

This is to speak of literature at its highest; and with the four great elders who are still spared to our respect and admiration, with Carlyle, Ruskin, Browning, and Tennyson before us, it would be cowardly to consider it at first in any lesser aspect. But while we cannot follow these athletes, while we may none of us, perhaps, be very vigorous, very original, or very wise, I still contend that, in the humblest sort of literary work, we have it in our power either to do great harm or great good. We may seek merely to please; we may seek, having no higher gift, merely to gratify the idle nine days' curiosity of our contemporaries; or we may essay, however feebly, to instruct. In each of these we shall have to deal with that remarkable art of words which, because it is the dialect of life,

THE MORALITY OF THE PROFESSION OF LETTERS   103

comes home so easily and powerfully to the minds of men; and since that is so, we contribute, in each of these branches, to build up the sum of sentiments and appreciations which goes by the name of Public Opinion or Public Feeling. The total of a nation's reading, in these days of daily papers, greatly modifies the total of the nation's speech; and the speech and reading, taken together, form the efficient educational medium of youth. A good man or woman may keep a youth some little while in clearer air; but the contemporary atmosphere is all-powerful in the end on the average of mediocre characters. The copious Corinthian baseness of the American reporter or the Parisian *chroniquer*, both so lightly readable, must exercise an incalculable influence for ill; they touch upon all subjects, and on all with the same ungenerous hand; they begin the consideration of all, in young and unprepared minds, in an unworthy spirit; on all, they supply some pungency for dull people to quote. The mere body of this ugly matter overwhelms the rare utterances of good men; the sneering, the selfish, and the cowardly are scattered in broad sheets on every table, while the antidote, in small volumes, lies unread upon the shelf. I have spoken of the American and the French, not because they are so much baser, but so much more readable, than the English; their evil is done more effectively, in America for the masses, in French for the few that care to read; but with us as with them, the duties of literature are daily neglected, truth daily perverted and suppressed, and grave subjects daily degraded in the treatment. The journalist is not reckoned an important officer; yet judge of the good he might do, the harm he does; judge of it by one instance only: that when we find two journals on the reverse sides of politics each, on the same day, openly garbling a piece of news for the interest of its own party, we smile at the discovery (no discovery now!) as over a good joke and pardonable stratagem. Lying so open is scarce lying, it is true, but one of the things that we profess to teach our young is a respect for truth; and I cannot think this piece of education will be crowned with any great success, so long as some of us practise and the rest openly approve of public falsehood.

There are two duties incumbent upon any man who enters on

the business of writing: truth to the fact and a good spirit in the treatment. In every department of literature, though so low as hardly to deserve the name, truth to the fact is of importance to the education and comfort of mankind, and so hard to preserve, that the faithful trying to do so will lend some dignity to the man who tries it. Our judgments are based upon two things: first, upon the original preferences of our soul; but, second, upon the mass of testimony to the nature of God, man, and the universe which reaches us, in divers manners, from without. For the most part these divers manners are reducible to one, all that we learn of past times and much that we learn of our own reaching us through the medium of books or papers, and even he who cannot read learning from the same source at second-hand and by the report of him who can. Thus the sum of the contemporary knowledge or ignorance of good and evil is, in large measure, the handiwork of those who write. Those who write have to see that each man's knowledge is, as near as they can make it, answerable to the facts of life; that he shall not suppose himself an angel or a monster; nor take this world for a hell; nor be suffered to imagine that all rights are concentred in his own caste or country, or all veracities in his own parochial creed. Each man should learn what is within him, that he may strive to mend; he must be taught what is without him, that he may be kind to others. It can never be wrong to tell him the truth; for, in his disputable state, weaving as he goes his theory of life, steering himself, cheering or reproving others, all facts are of the first importance to his conduct; and even if a fact shall discourage or corrupt him, it is still best that he should know it; for it is in this world as it is, and not in a world made easy by educational suppressions, that he must win his way to shame or glory. In one word, it must always be foul to tell what is false; and it can never be safe to suppress what is true. The very fact that you omit may be the fact which somebody was wanting, for one man's meat is another man's poison, and I have known a person who was cheered by the perusal of *Candide*. Every fact is a part of that great puzzle we must set together; and none that comes directly in a writer's path but has some nice relations, unperceivable by him, to the totality and bearing of the subject under hand. Yet there are

THE MORALITY OF THE PROFESSION OF LETTERS   105

certain classes of fact eternally more necessary than others, and it is with these that literature must first bestir itself. They are not hard to distinguish, nature once more easily leading us; for the necessary, because the efficacious, facts are those which are most interesting to the natural mind of man. Those which are coloured, picturesque, human, and rooted in morality, and those, on the other hand, which are clear, indisputable, and a part of science, are alone vital in importance, seizing by their interest, or useful to communicate. So far as the writer merely narrates, he should principally tell of these. He should tell of the kind and wholesome and beautiful elements of our life; he should tell unsparingly of the evil and sorrow of the present, to move us with instances; he should tell of wise and good people in the past, to excite us by example; and of these he should tell soberly and truthfully, not glossing faults, that we may neither grow discouraged with our-selves nor exacting to our neighbours. So the body of contem-porary literature, ephemeral and feeble in itself, touches in the minds of men the springs of thought and kindness, and supports them (for those who will go at all are easily supported) on their way to what is true and right. And if, in any degree, it does so now, how much more might it do so if the writers chose! There is not a life in all the records of the past but, properly studied, might lend a hint and a help to some contemporary. There is not a juncture in to-day's affairs but some useful word may yet be said of it. Even the reporter has an office, and, with clear eyes and honest language, may unveil injustices and point the way to progress. And for a last word: in all narration there is only one way to be clever, and that is to be exact. To be vivid is a secondary quality which must presuppose the first; for vividly to convey a wrong impression is only to make failure conspicuous.

But a fact may be viewed on many sides; it may be chronicled with rage, tears, laughter, indifference, or admiration, and by each of these the story will be transformed to something else. The newspapers that told of the return of our representatives from Berlin, even if they had not differed as to the facts, would have sufficiently differed by their spirits; so that the one description would have been a second ovation, and the other a prolonged insult. The subject makes but a trifling part of any piece of literature, and the view of the writer is itself a fact more important because less disputable than the others. Now this spirit in which a subject is regarded, important in all kinds of literary work, becomes all-important in works of fiction, meditation, or rhapsody; for there it not only colours but itself chooses the facts; not only modifies but shapes the work. And hence, over the far larger proportion of the field of literature, the health or disease of the writer's mind or momentary humour forms not only the leading feature of his work, but is, at bottom, the only thing he can communicate to others. In all works of art, widely speaking, it is first of all the author's attitude that is narrated, though in the attitude there be implied a whole experience and a theory of life. An author who has begged the question and reposes in some narrow faith cannot, if he would, express the whole or even many of the sides of this various existence; for, his own life being maim, some of them are not admitted in his theory, and were only dimly and unwillingly recognised in his experience. Hence the smallness, the triteness, and the inhumanity in works of merely sectarian religion; and hence we find equal although unsimilar limitation in works inspired by the spirit of the flesh or the despicable taste for high society. So that the first duty of any man who is to write is intellectual. Designedly or not, he has so far set himself up for a leader of the minds of men; and he must see that his own mind is kept supple, charitable, and bright. Everything but prejudice should find a voice through him; he should see the good in all things; where he has even a fear that he does not wholly under-stand, there he should be wholly silent; and he should recognise from the first that he has only one tool in his workshop, and that tool is sympathy.

The second duty, far harder to define, is moral. There are a thousand different humours in the mind, and about each of them, when it is uppermost, some literature tends to be deposited. Is this to be allowed? Not certainly in every case, and yet perhaps in more than rigourists would fancy. It were to be desired that all literary work, and chiefly works of art, issued from sound, human, healthy, and potent impulses, whether grave or laughing, humorous,

THE MORALITY OF THE PROFESSION OF LETTERS 107

romantic or religious. Yet it cannot be denied that some valuable books are partially insane; some, mostly religious, partially inhuman; and very many tainted with morbidity and impotence. We do not loathe a masterpiece although we gird against its blemishes. We are not, above all, to look for faults, but merits. There is no book perfect, even in design; but there are many that will delight, improve, or encourage the reader. On the one hand, the Hebrew psalms are the only religious poetry on earth; yet they contain sallies that savour rankly of the man of blood. On the other hand, Alfred de Musset had a poisoned and a contorted nature; I am only quoting that generous and frivolous giant, old Dumas, when I accuse him of a bad heart; yet when the impulse under which he wrote was purely creative, he could give us works like *Carmosine* or *Fantasio*, in which the last note of the romantic comedy seems to have been found again to touch and please us. When Flaubert wrote *Madame Bovary*, I believe he thought chiefly of a somewhat morbid realism; and behold! the book turned in his hands into a masterpiece of appalling morality. But the truth is, when books are conceived under a great stress, with a soul of ninefold power, nine times heated and electrified by effort, the conditions of our being are seized with such an ample grasp, that, even should the main design be trivial or base, some truth and beauty cannot fail to be expressed. Out of the strong comes forth sweetness; but an ill thing poorly done is an ill thing top and bottom. And so this can be no encouragement to knock-kneed, feeble-wristed scribes, who must take their business conscientiously or be ashamed to practise it.

Man is imperfect; yet, in his literature, he must express himself and his own views and preferences; for to do anything else is to do a far more perilous thing than to risk being immoral: it is to be sure of being untrue. To ape a sentiment, even a good one, is to travesty a sentiment; that will not be helpful. To conceal a sentiment, if you are sure you hold it, is to take a liberty with truth. There is probably no point of view possible to a sane man but contains some truth and, in the true connection, might be profitable to the race. I am not afraid of the truth, if any one could tell it me, but I am afraid of parts of it impertinently uttered. There is a time to dance and a time to mourn; to be harsh as well as to be sentimental; to be ascetic as well as to glorify the appetites; and if a man were to combine all these extremes into his work, each in its place and proportion, that work would be the world's masterpiece of morality, as well as of art. Partiality is immorality; for any book is wrong that gives a misleading picture of the world and life. The trouble is that the weakling must be partial; the work of one proving dank and depressing; of another, cheap and vulgar; of a third, epileptically sensual; of a fourth, sourly ascetic. In literature as in conduct, you can never hope to do exactly right. All you can do is to make as sure as possible; and for that there is but one rule. Nothing should be done in a hurry that can be done slowly. It is no use to write a book and put it by for nine or even ninety years; for in the writing you will have partly convinced yourself; the delay must precede any beginning; and if you meditate a work of art, you should first long roll the subject under the tongue to make sure you like the flavour, before you brew a volume that shall taste of it from end to end; or if you propose to enter on the field of controversy, you should first have thought upon the question under all conditions, in health as well as in sickness, in sorrow as well as in joy. It is this nearness of examination necessary for any true and kind writing, that makes the practice of the art a prolonged and noble education for the writer.

There is plenty to do, plenty to say, or to say over again, in the meantime. Any literary work which conveys faithful facts or pleasing impressions is a service to the public. It is even a service to be thankfully proud of having rendered. The slightest novels are a blessing to those in distress, not chloroform itself a greater. Our fine old sea-captain's life was justified when Carlyle soothed his mind with *The King's Own* or *Newton Forster*. To please is to serve; and so far from its being difficult to instruct while you amuse, it is difficult to do the one thoroughly without the other. Some part of the writer or his life will crop out in even a vapid book; and to read a novel that was conceived with any force is to multiply experience and to exercise the sympathies. Every article, every piece of verse, every essay, every *entre-filet*, is destined to pass, however swiftly, through the minds of some portion of the

THE MORALITY OF THE PROFESSION OF LETTERS 109

public, and to colour, however transiently, their thoughts. When any subject falls to be discussed, some scribbler on a paper has the invaluable opportunity of beginning its discussion in a dignified and human spirit; and if there were enough who did so in our public press, neither the public nor the Parliament would find it in their minds to drop to meaner thoughts. The writer has the chance to stumble, by the way, on something pleasing, something interesting, something encouraging, were it only to a single reader. He will be unfortunate, indeed, if he suit no one. He has the chance, besides, to stumble on something that a dull person shall be able to comprehend; and for a dull person to have read anything and, for that once, comprehended it, makes a marking epoch in his education.

Here, then, is work worth doing and worth trying to do well. And so, if I were minded to welcome any great accession to our trade, it should not be from any reason of a higher wage, but because it was a trade which was useful in a very great and in a very high degree; which every honest tradesman could make more serviceable to mankind in his single strength; which was difficult to do well and possible to do better every year; which called for scrupulous thought on the part of all who practised it, and hence became a perpetual education to their nobler natures; and which, pay it as you please, in the large majority of the best cases will still be underpaid. For surely at this time of day in the nineteenth century, there is nothing that an honest man should fear more timorously than getting and spending more than he deserves.

Achevé d'imprimer par l'Imprimerie Floch à Mayenne, le 10 janvier 2005.
Dépôt légal : janvier 2005 - N° d'impression : 61960 - ISBN : 2-84304-289-5
Imprimé en France